He was learning too much about her

"What's made you so afraid of this, Antonia? It's the most natural thing in the world...."

"I don't want to have an affair with you. I don't sleep with every man I'm attracted to—I have standards, and quick, easy affairs are not my style."

"I'm not angling for a quick, easy affair. I'm not in the habit of sleeping with women I don't know and like and trust."

"So you'll get to know me, and then when you decide you like and trust me, you'll sleep with me," she said furiously. "How kind!"

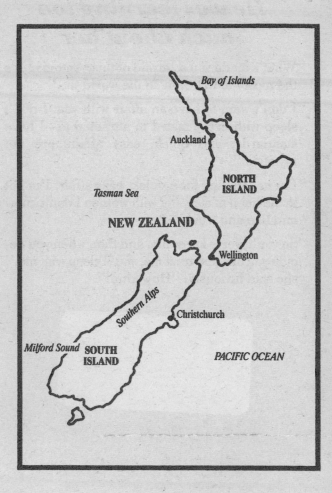

ROBYN DONALD

Such Dark Magic

Harlequin Books

TORONTO • NEW YORK • LONDON
AMSTERDAM • PARIS • SYDNEY • HAMBURG
STOCKHOLM • ATHENS • TOKYO • MILAN
MADRID • WARSAW • BUDAPEST • AUCKLAND

The Oral Historians in this book
bear absolutely no resemblance whatsoever
to the two Oral Historians I know and
thank, Megan and Sarah.

ISBN 0-373-11611-X

SUCH DARK MAGIC

CHAPTER ONE

WHEN Antonia Ridd arrived at the office late on Monday morning after a particularly arduous interview with a deaf old lady and her asthmatic cat, it took only one glance at her assistant to warn of trouble. Antonia's violet eyes, so dark that most people didn't realise their true colour, rested thoughtfully on Heather's face. Hunched over the computer keyboard, the younger woman kept her head down, but she couldn't hide the guilty flush creeping up her throat.

Concerned, Antonia asked, 'What's the matter?'

'I'm all right,' Heather mumbled.

Antonia's brown brows climbed, but she nodded. 'I'll believe you. Still, if whatever is making you look so green gets any worse, you'd better take the rest of the day off.'

'Oh, thanks,' Heather said, with a spurt of her normal spirit.

Antonia's small perfect cupid's bow of a mouth, the bane of her life, quirked into an ironic smile. 'Any time.'

She sat down at the desk provided by the trust that had set up the Oral History Unit eighteen months before in response to a millionaire's bequest, and flicked a silky white-blonde tress back from her face. Most people assumed it was bleached, but, along with the dark lashes that surrounded her eyes, her pale hair was entirely natural.

After a quick, frowning glance at the calendar she began to check the rest of her appointments for the day. There was only a preliminary interview late in the afternoon, which meant she could get on with some of the eternal letter-writing, as well as index a few tapes. And she had notes to work on for a talk she was delivering at the end of the week.

Only a month to go and she'd be off on holiday. As she reached for her notes she smiled; her job was one in a million, but the prospect of a fortnight spent wandering through Northland, with several long, lovely days at Tiffany's and Eliot's bach to finish up with, was more than a little alluring.

'Antonia,' Heather said suddenly, her voice thin and strained.

'Mmm?'

'Philip Angove's coming to see you today.'

Antonia shot her a startled look. 'Is he?' she said after a moment, when it was clear Heather expected some answer.

Sir Edward Angove had bequeathed the money to set up the unit. When Antonia had been interviewed for this job, Philip, his nephew and the sole remaining Angove, was overseas with a trade mission; for a variety of reasons she had never met him, but it was clear from everyone's respectful manner whenever his name came up that he cast a long shadow.

At the sudden, peremptory tattoo on the door Heather gave a squeak, hastily cut short.

'The Demon King arrives,' Antonia said frivolously. Her cat-slanted eyes hardened as they scanned Heather's appalled face. Clearly whatever had been worrying Heather was bound up with Philip Angove's unexpected arrival.

An instinctive feminine impulse led to a quick personal check. Antonia straightened her shirtwaister, timeless and modest in fine cotton. Its colours, violet and lilac, emphasised the intense violet of her eyes, and the softly bloused style reduced her somewhat too ample bust to proportion with her height, barely five feet three, and covered up the narrow waist that made her breasts so obvious.

With a nod that freed her hair from its starkly geometric cut and set it swirling around her small pointed face, Antonia exhaled a deep, calming breath. 'Well, what are you waiting for? Let the man in.'

Heather said, 'Antonia——'

'Don't keep him hovering outside. I imagine he's not used to it. Being a multi-millionaire and all.'

Still looking hunted—almost frightened—Heather hesitated, then gave Antonia an imploring look and went across to open the door. 'Oh, Mr Angove,' she said, a note of open appreciation warming her voice as she directed a smile eight inches or so upwards.

'Heather.' The voice was deep and crisp and authoritative.

Antonia looked from one face to the other, her assistant's adoring, almost simpering, the strong, hawklike features of the man relaxing into a smile that had something of the paternal about it. One of the reasons Heather had been appointed to the position was that she had grown up on the Angove station. Although Philip Angove had nothing to do with the unit, or the trustees that oversaw it, he had the clout to insist on that.

The younger woman had proved her worth in the unit, so it had been some time since Antonia had thought of the connection. It did, however, explain how Heather knew he was coming in. She had spent the weekend at home.

'I'll see you later,' Philip Angove said now. 'I want to see Miss Ridd alone, if I may.'

A chill of foreboding chased its way down Antonia's spine. Picking up her pen again, she looked blindly down at her desk.

'Yes, of course. Antonia,' Heather breathed, 'Mr Angove's here.'

Antonia got to her feet and walked towards him while he held the door open for Heather with an authority that was as effortless as it was arrogant. 'Come in, Mr Angove,' she said politely as the younger woman left without a backward glance.

The approaching man took up far more space than his height and rangy build should allow, although he had to be about six feet two, and his shoulders were definitely in proportion.

He seemed to walk in an aura of crackling energy as he came towards her with a smooth litheness based on great strength and the constant use of it. Black hair waved in an ordered fashion over an arrogantly poised head, and autocratic, aquiline features were highlighted by olive skin. Curiously pale eyes, an unusual green, burned like flames in the dark austerity of his face. As he got closer Antonia realised that they were flecked with gold.

With no pretence of circumspection he scrutinised her. In the warm bright light she could see the shadow of his long, straight eyelashes on the stark bones of his cheeks. They should have allayed the fierce angularity of his face, but they didn't. It would take infinitely more than the softness of lashes to temper the bone-structure that turned Philip Angove's face into a blade, strong and striking.

He looked at her as though she was something he had hoped never to see, his glance swinging from her face to her hands, where it rested for a split second before returning. Checking to see whether she was married, Antonia decided resentfully.

She stiffened, her pointed chin jutting, but the insulting survey continued until eventually the crystalline gaze stopped for an endless second on her mouth.

Cynicism compressed its well-defined bow. Men seemed to like looking at her mouth, so surprisingly lush in her small face. Its shape, with connotations of jazz and flappers and the Roaring Twenties when gentlemen preferred blondes, used to drive her crazy, but she had long ago learned to suppress the embarrassment it caused her. Now she even wore lipstick that emphasised its curvy, precisely cut contours.

Almost immediately his gaze flicked upwards, piercing through her soul, plumbing the opaque violet of her eyes in a glance as swift as it was intimidating. Helplessly, Antonia stared back. He smiled, and the hair on the back of her neck lifted.

Instinct told Antonia to get the hell out of there, *now*, right *now*.

For there was no warmth in his expression. Very white teeth showed an instant in a naked statement of aggression before the smile vanished. Green-gold lights gleamed beneath the black lashes. Philip Angove's beautiful mouth, a thin upper lip sculpted over the full, ambiguous arc of the lower, hardened into a straight line.

'Miss Ridd,' he said smoothly. 'So we meet at last. How do you do?'

'How do you do?' She didn't want to extend her hand, but custom and habit dictated that she do it. Lean, tanned fingers closed firmly around her slender, pale ones. Although he was dressed in formal business clothes the tell-tale calluses indicated a man who spent much of his time working with his hands.

Electricity ran up Antonia's arm, scorching through every cell, every nerve-end in her body in such an intense physical reaction that she thought she could hear the sharp crack and fizz, smell the tang of the ozone.

Transfixed, she watched the iris of Philip Angove's eyes narrow to a luminous jade ring around the dilated pupils. In spite of her bewilderment she was rocked by a deep, savage, dangerous pleasure, because he felt it too, that primitive rake of desire.

Of course he had recognised it before she did. More experience, no doubt. He had that air of accomplishment, of sensual knowledge. Jealousy, wild and primal as the attraction, combined with Antonia's instinctive wariness to form a volatile cocktail of emotions. Hastily stepping back, she put several feet between them and saw him win his own battle, reimposing once more the concentrated authority of his will over that untamed response.

Antonia refused to utter the words that trembled on her tongue, stupid words, any words to fill that taut emptiness. Instead she concentrated on manufacturing a steely resistance to his particular brand of masculinity.

With the result that when he spoke she couldn't stop a small start of shock.

'I assume you know why I'm here.'

'No,' she retorted, unable to hide the defensive note in her voice.

'If you'll sit down,' he said with a courtesy that further ruffled her, 'I'll tell you.'

He waited until she was seated before folding his lean body into a chair. Without preamble he began, 'I've been told that you interviewed a woman who told you a piece of gossip—untrue gossip—about my parents.'

It had to be Mrs Collins.

Antonia's eyes heated like smouldering violets. The reason for Heather's unusual demeanour was now explained. How dared she? 'Heather had no right to tell you that,' she said stiffly. 'Her loyalty should have been to this unit.'

'Her loyalty to my family is of older duration.' The words were cold and distinct, underlined by a note of warning. Clearly he had no intention of allowing Heather to suffer for her disloyalty. He waited for a moment, but, when Antonia made no reply, continued crisply, 'As it happens, Heather didn't tell me. She was worried about it, because of course she knew it wasn't true, so she consulted her parents. They told me. Miss Ridd, I want that tape erased.'

'I'm afraid I can't do that.' With a fervent hope that none of her inner turmoil was apparent, Antonia drew a deep breath, facing his hard, unsmiling survey with as much equanimity as she could produce. She had no idea whether Mrs Collins's revelations were true or not, but that made no difference to the value of the tape. She was about to explain when he spoke.

'The information you were given is totally false. The woman who repeated it to you is a pathetic creature who blames my family for the death of her daughter thirty-three years ago. She set this whole fabrication going then, but was—persuaded,' his voice altered fractionally, 'to stop it. Apparently she believes it's safe to start the whole sordid fantasy up again now. My uncle didn't leave the money to set up this unit to have it propagate lies and innuendoes that Elva Collins didn't dare repeat while he was alive.'

Antonia swallowed. The intimidation was overt and uncompromising, but she made a measured reply. 'I can't erase the tapes, or even edit them, because under Sir Edward Angove's bequest this unit was set up to collect information that will go into an archive, a repository for people's memories. Even when we know facts to be untrue we leave them; what we are trying to build up is a living history of what was said and thought and experienced at that time. Gossip has as much relevance as the historical truth, if it was believed to be true, and if people acted on it.'

'But this is patently and unarguably false,' he said inflexibly. 'Apart from that, it's not important to anyone but my family.'

Antonia's chin lifted. 'I'm sorry,' she said, her voice soft and cool and just as inflexible. 'If it became known that we edited the tapes people would have every right to refuse to talk to us. Your uncle himself formulated the rules and guidelines we work with.'

Broad shoulders lifted, not giving an inch. He watched her from narrowed eyes as he said, 'He was an Angove; he'd have had this building burned to the ground before he let filthy lies like that be used against him. It was a good try, Miss Ridd, but it's not going to work. I want that tape erased.'

He couldn't do this! Driven back on her heels, Antonia said stiffly, 'Then I'm afraid you must accept my resignation. I can't be a party to censorship.'

And knew that she had surprised him. It was her face, of course, those irritatingly doll-like, delicate features, combined with her pale hair and a gently voluptuous figure, that made men think she was an empty-headed little blonde, easily manipulated and influenced. She rather enjoyed disabusing them of this illusion.

Philip Angove's straight black brows drew together. 'So you're going to give up your career? There's not much call for your particular talents in a country as small as New Zealand, surely, and the competition is quite fierce. Oral history's fashionable just now. What are you going to do if you storm out in high dudgeon?'

Driven by incredulity and rage, she sprang to her feet, instantly regretting her impetuous movement when he too stood, towering over her in a way that reminded her unpleasantly of Bryan, also secure and confident in his wealth and social position. But she had been a naïve eighteen when she burned her fingers on Bryan Howard; nine extra years had given her the self-confidence to deal with any man.

'That,' she retorted icily, 'is my business. And if you think you can get any ethical historian to accept a job where they're going to have to erase any tapes that upset certain people, I'm afraid you will find out your mistake. Now——'

In a calm, judicious voice, he interrupted, 'Aren't you being rather hasty?'

'No, I'm not, I'm never——' she began incautiously, but the hurrying words died unborn at the lift of his brows.

'No?' he said, his voice mockingly amused.

'No.' She took a deep breath, willing her voice to remain firm. 'Now, if you'll excuse me, Mr Angove, I have things to do.'

'Like writing a letter of resignation,' he said, and suddenly smiled. That smile summoned a sexual charisma that blazed forth, almost violent in its impact, swamping her in its intense forcefield. And beside the hard mouth with its equivocal lower lip there appeared a dimple.

Fascinated, Antonia stared. It was so completely incongruous. A dimple should have eased the uncompromising contours of his mouth, but it didn't. Instead, it accented them, just as the long sweep of his lashes emphasised the high, arrogant cheekbones.

He glanced down at his watch, a thin gold thing on a tanned wrist that looked as strong as steel. 'Perhaps I've been too hasty. Can I take you out to lunch, where we can discuss things in a more civilised fashion?'

Horrified by her weak impulse to acquiesce, Antonia shook her head stubbornly. 'There's nothing to discuss. You gave me a direct order, which I refused to carry out. You threatened me with the loss of my job, so I'll resign.'

'I think,' he said, smiling sardonically, 'that both of us may have let the heat of the moment overcome common sense. You should at least listen to my reasons for wanting that tape erased, and you can do that over lunch.'

She stared at him, sensing an implacable will. After a moment she said steadily, 'Mr Angove, I know the reason, and I understand your reaction. Believe me, taking me out to lunch is not going to make any difference.'

His smile echoed the confidence of a man who knew that he was attractive, a man who used his charm so effortlessly that he probably wasn't even aware he had it. Alarm bells jangled. Bryan had used to smile at her like that.

'I don't want to see you resigning on a point of principle when perhaps a discussion over a meal can help. Come on.'

What harm could he do? She was well armoured against men like this. And it might get him off her back.

She smiled too, hiding her contempt, and said pleasantly, 'Very well, but I am not going to change my mind.'

'I'm going to do my best to persuade you to,' he said, just as pleasantly, but with a hard note underlying the words.

It took only a moment to set the answerphone and pick up her bag. Without speaking he strode beside her down the corridors of the museum, chilly even now.

The foyer of the Greek Revival building was packed with tourists milling about, some going in, some coming out, and all, Antonia thought acidly, with a glance to spare for the man who cleared a path through them by the sheer force of his personality.

Antonia didn't like crowds, they made her edgy, but the nervous tension that racked her now was not caused by the people jostling around them.

Once out from the shelter of the huge pillared portico she exhaled sharply and frowned at a sky hazed with translucent white cloud that did nothing to temper the heat.

'Are you all right?' Philip Angove asked suddenly.

Startled, her eyes flashed up to a dark, frowning face. Hastily she looked away again. She wouldn't have expected him to be so perceptive, but obviously he had the keen, quick instincts of a predator. 'I'm fine,' she said politely, ignoring, as he did, the open appreciation in the faces of two exquisite Japanese women as they rejoined their tourist bus.

He opened the door of a Mercedes Benz, a sleek silver monster all leather and luxury inside, which he had left in the director's parking space.

'It's a wonder you didn't get a ticket,' she said lightly.

His cheeks creased into a smile. 'My father was a friend of his,' he told her.

Naturally.

In the car Antonia clasped her hands lightly together and concentrated on looking away from the incisive angles and lines of Philip Angove's autocratic profile, rigidly quelling the inner turmoil that was doing its best to destroy her hard-won composure. Unfortunately, even with her eyes directed firmly to the left, she could still see his lean, tanned hands on the wheel, competent and strong as he drove through the Domain and then down into Auckland's jammed streets. The traffic held no terrors for him, but then he lived only an hour or so's drive away, and, according to Heather, was often in Auckland.

Not, Antonia decided acidly, your normal farmer.

She dredged up more information that Heather had imparted. The original Angove, an Englishman, had decided in the 1870s to chance his luck in the colonies. He had chosen to settle on the shores of the Kaipara Harbour, north-west of Auckland. Perhaps it was the traditional new chum's luck that had led him to buy the huge tract of land from the Maori tribe who owned the area, land which had been in the hands of his descendants ever since. In subsequent years the family had prospered immensely, as well as playing an important role in the affairs of their new country.

Antonia wished that she had listened more carefully to the worshipful Heather. There was nothing like knowing your adversary to give you an advantage.

In the meantime she set herself to stiffening her resolve. Of course this invitation to lunch was part of a softening-up process. When Philip Angove had realised she wasn't going to buckle under he'd decided to see how charm and sweet persuasion worked. No doubt he intended to dazzle her with virile masculine magnetism until eventually she agreed to bargain. Possibly he would settle on asking her to edit the tape—under his supervision of course!

Antonia sent another swift glance at his slashing profile. He looked as though he had been making deals since childhood, and losing on very few of them.

A needle of excitement pierced her body, but was immediately banished. Philip Angove had probably never had a woman say no to him and mean it, but she would have to, because her integrity was more important to her than pandering to his potent charisma.

He drove into an underground car park, pulling up in another place marked with a director's sign.

Without thinking Antonia murmured, 'Was your father a friend of this director's, too?'

His teeth showed white for a moment in the darkness of his face. 'No, this space belongs to me.'

Which suitably squashed her. Once out, he took her elbow in a light grip and guided her across the floor to the lift. His cool fingers on her bare skin sent tiny sparks of awareness roaring out of control through her.

This, Antonia thought with a quick, exasperated panic, was physical attraction, a conflagration of wildfire, based on nothing but chemistry, dying as swiftly as it had been born. She had experienced it once before, although it hadn't been as—uncontrollable as this, but then Bryan Howard hadn't been as formidable as Philip Angove. Never would be too soon to feel it again. Yet pulling out of his grasp could only make him aware of her reaction. It took self-control to suffer his touch, but she gritted her teeth and waited until they were in the lift before moving away from him.

Eight storeys up, when they stepped out of the lift, he did it again; apparently he was in the habit of steering women around. How many, she thought with a flash of truculent resentment, had he set alight? Instinct warned her that it was almost certainly too many.

The restaurant was one she recognised, although she had never been there. Always counted in the top three in Auckland, it was as expensive as it was well known. Antonia looked down at her pretty, unremarkable shirt-waister, fighting the shaming impulse to turn tail.

Of course he was known there, and of course he was shown immediately to a table by the windows, with a magnificent view out across the lambent, smooth waters of the Waitemata Harbour. The waitress who unfolded the stiff linen napkins and arranged them on their laps knew him too; the smile she directed at him was warm, with a sliver of purely feminine appreciation laced through the respect.

'Nice to see you again, Mr Angove,' she said. 'Are you off to see a show today?'

His answering smile was a masterpiece. Antonia didn't blame the woman for her complete capitulation to that sudden, potent charm. Does he even know he's doing it? she wondered morosely.

'No, not this time,' he said in a pleasant, impersonal tone. 'We'll have the menu straight away, as Miss Ridd has only a short lunch-hour.'

The waitress was far too well trained to reveal anything other than polite interest when she smiled at Antonia, but Antonia knew that she had noted the shirt-waister and the total lack of style or money in her clothes, and had dismissed her accordingly. No doubt she was used to seeing Philip Angove with sleek designer women, beautiful and expensive and sophisticated.

The old humiliation came welling up, corroding and blackening her mood, but she vanquished it. She was not going to let herself be sucked back into that swamp of inferiority and self-pity.

Crisply, she said as soon as the waitress had gone, 'Mr Angove, I'm not going to give in, even if it does mean losing my job. And all the charm in the world, however formidable, isn't going to make me change my mind.'

The gold was suddenly leached from his eyes, so that all that showed behind his thick lashes were glinting green crystals. 'I'm glad,' he said softly, leaning back to survey her with a smile that was as dangerous as his former anger had been, 'that you consider me to have charm. At least I haven't queered my pitch beyond repair. But we'll talk about the problem later. Tell me a little about yourself.'

Of course he didn't want to know about Antonia Ridd, whose only claim to fame was that she had eyes the same colour as Elizabeth Taylor's. However, it was easier to take him at his word, so she said politely enough, 'I'm not very interesting, I'm afraid.'

'I'll be the judge of that.'

Patronising swine! Deliberately making her voice monotonous, she said, 'I grew up on the West Coast, on a dairy farm. My father was a farm worker.'

Until he had skipped the country and left her and her mother penniless and alone. After that her mother had taken refuge from grief in alcohol and bitterness and men, eventually running herself into a telephone pole one dark night. Antonia had lived with her best friend's family then, finding a job in the office of the local garage after she had left school. Just after her eighteenth birthday Bryan Howard had arrived home from four years spent overseas, and that meeting had set her life on a totally different path from the one she had always envisaged.

'If I remember correctly form your c.v. you went to Otago University.'

'Yes.' Sheer bloody-mindedness and a bitter refusal to be a victim like her mother, as well as a strong desire to show the Howards that she could make something of her life, had sent her to university.

'I majored in history,' she said, smiling impersonally, 'and after I got an MA I found work in the Oral History Unit at Wellington. From there I came up to Auckland to this job——'

'Ah, thought it was you, Philip,' a cheerful male voice broke in.

The interrupter was a middle-aged man, lean and ruddy of face, dressed in dark, well cut business clothes. With him was a pretty woman ten years or so younger, wearing an exquisitely designed suit of clear red with one of the fashionable new shorter skirts. Very chic, Antonia thought pensively. Both newcomers smiled at Philip, who got to his feet and accepted a kiss from the woman after shaking the man's hand.

That done, both turned their attention to her with identical looks of well hidden interest as Philip introduced her.

'Ah, of course,' Maddie Traile said, and smiled at her, not exactly condescendingly but rather in the manner of a woman asking a child whether she was enjoying a treat. 'Such an interesting job! And such a wonderful idea of your uncle's, Philip.'

'He felt very strongly that a nation's history is as important as its geography,' Philip responded.

This produced a respectful assent. Both Maddie and her husband, it transpired, were lawyers in a high-powered firm in Queen Street. They talked of people they all knew, until Maddie said sweetly, 'Philip, my love, why don't you come to our party tomorrow night? Do say you will—it's going to be great fun, and there's always room for you, you know. I'd have asked you sooner, only I thought you were in Indonesia on some dreary old government mission.'

Suave, Antonia decided snidely, was the only word to describe his smile.

'Well, Antonia,' he said, ignoring completely the stunned surprise in Maddie Traile's face, 'shall we go to a party tomorrow night?'

He was punishing Maddie for being rude. Yet there was a glitter of gold in his gaze that both challenged and provoked Antonia.

She said coolly, 'No, I'm sorry, I'm already going out tomorrow night.'

Philip turned and smiled at the suddenly self-conscious woman beside him, who was standing with her mouth slightly open. 'Sorry, Maddie, but we can't make it.'

'Oh, what a pity! Next time, perhaps.' Outwardly she had regained her poise, but unease flickered in her eyes in spite of the smile she bestowed on him.

As well it might, Antonia thought drily. It was the height of rudeness to ask one of a couple out and not the other, even if the couple were the barest acquaintances, and Philip Angove had made sure Maddie Traile realised it.

However, Philip's answering smile was enigmatic and bland; he let the wretched woman kiss him goodbye, shook hands with Jeremy, and sat down again.

'I'm sorry about that,' he said calmly.

'Was your father a friend of his too?' she asked, a saccharine sweetness barely coating each crisp word.

His answering grin was swift and amused. 'No, my father had little patience with the Trailes of this world. But Jeremy's an amiable chap. I've known him for years. And they are both very good at their jobs.'

Which seemed to be important to him. Clearly he didn't suffer fools gladly. On the other hand, neither was he tolerant of bad manners.

'Why didn't you want to go?' he asked lazily.

She froze, aware that her expression had given her away. Her mind scurried around until she finally managed to say with what she hoped was something like poise, 'I don't know them, and I wasn't invited, as you well know. She asked you.'

'Yes,' he said calmly. 'She has no breeding, Maddie, and sometimes it shows.'

How Antonia hated that word! It echoed hideously in her mind, bringing with it her personal experience of people like Philip Angove, who thought breeding was all.

Bryan Howard had been one of them. He never did anything so vulgar as shout when he lost his temper. In a voice as smooth as silk he had said, 'You're just a nobody, with no breeding, no manners, nothing but your face and your breasts and your willingness to open your legs to recommend you.'

She had had nine years' practice in fighting those memories. Her face remained blank.

Until Philip Angove said blandly, 'And, of course, she is insecure enough to see any other beautiful woman as a threat.'

Antonia couldn't prevent the quick shock that flashed across her small features, or the sudden distaste that followed it. He recognised both emotions, of course; he was watching her from half-closed eyes, too carefully, too closely for her peace of mind. No doubt each fleeting expression, every moment of hesitation, was being filed away in that shrewd, dangerously quick brain, ready to be used as ammunition against her if the time should come when he needed it.

She had to get through lunch as well as she could, and then, she promised herself, she wasn't ever going to have anything to do with Philip Angove again.

'So you don't believe you are beautiful,' he said quietly, his eyes roving her features with slow, mocking appreciation. 'Not in the normal manner, I'll admit, but that mouth is maddening, and unless you wear coloured contact lenses——'

'I don't!' Hot colour flamed across her cheekbones and she was unable to drag her gaze away from the unsparing demand of his gaze.

'Then those eyes are the most fascinating I've ever seen. And your hair is the colour of moonlight on white roses.'

There was a curious purring quality in his voice that should have sounded sensual but which succeeded only in reinforcing her sense of entrapment. At that moment, to Antonia's profound relief, the waitress arrived with the menus, and asked if they wanted a drink.

'Antonia?'

What was it you were advised to do if you were kidnapped? Make the people who held you recognise that you were human, so that it was more difficult for them to harm you. Perhaps if Philip Angove realised that she was a human being instead of someone to be threatened or charmed into submission it might help him see her point of view. And if all went well she would be able to keep both her integrity and her job.

'Orange juice,' she said quickly, when she realised that the waitress and Philip were both waiting for her to order.

She expected him to drink something alcoholic, but he surprised her by choosing mineral water, although the lunch he ordered was hearty enough. Clearly he worked hard on Motupipi; not even the superb cut of his charcoal suit could hide the almost violent masculinity, the coil and flexion of muscles strengthened by hours of back-breaking labour.

They talked of impersonal things during the meal, interrupted twice more by people who knew Philip, people with the same accent, the same gloss of sophistication, the same aura of money and assurance and social position.

Philip Angove's voice, his confidence and self-contained worldliness, abraded long-healed wounds, making Antonia more than ever determined not to give in to his charm.

'Something not right about the meal?' he enquired.

Antonia looked down at her chicken and avocado and mushroom salad. 'No,' she said quietly, 'it's quite delicious. Thank you.'

His smile was tinged with irony. 'But... ?'

Well, might as well give it to him. 'I keep waiting for the threats.'

He lifted one straight black brow; it seemed unconscious, but he did it with great effect. 'No threats,' he said. 'Only a request.'

'I won't change my mind,' she told him soberly. 'It's a matter of professional ethics.'

'I'd have thought that basic human ethics were more important than professional ones.'

Antonia winced, aware that he noted the tiny betrayal. 'I can understand how galling it must be,' she said, trying to sound businesslike, 'but it was your uncle who set up the unit, and he must have known the guidelines oral historians work to.'

Again that humourless smile, a mere movement of his lips. Antonia barely had time to regret the non-appearance of the dimple before his tone, detached yet inflexible, caught her attention.

'The last thing he intended was for the unit to be used as a base to propagate lies. Especially not about the family. His family name and reputation were infinitely important to him. As they are to me. Apart from that,' he finished relentlessly, 'I don't want my mother upset or worried any more by this. Her health is not the best.'

Antonia's head came up with a jerk. 'Surely Heather's parents didn't tell her, too?'

He showed his teeth. 'Elva Collins rang her up.'

'What?' Antonia stared at him. His hard-edged face was composed, but she sensed the dangerous emotions held in restraint only by his will, and her mouth went dry. After a moment she asked raggedly, 'Why on earth did she do that?'

'God knows. Oh, she's a true obsessive, normal in every other way but this. I feel sorry for her, but it doesn't make her actions any easier to cope with.'

Was he right? Elva Collins had seemed almost patently sane to Antonia. She asked quietly, 'Did she make *everything* up?'

His green eyes sharpened. 'I don't know exactly what happened. Naturally, my mother finds it difficult to talk about, even now. She says that Elva was driven temporarily insane by the death of her daughter, her only child. Kate Collins had been engaged to my uncle, who was a diplomat, but they broke it off, and apparently she took it very badly. She committed suicide a couple of months later. Uncle Edward was so upset by the whole affair that he never set foot in New Zealand again. There was gossip, of course, but it seems it was based on wild statements that Elva made after her daughter's death. She blamed my uncle, which was understandable, I suppose, but God alone knows what crazy logic persuaded her to drag my mother into it.'

The cold note in his voice sent a shiver across Antonia's skin. She nodded. It was more or less the same story she had heard from Elva Collins, except that Mrs Collins remained completely convinced that the engagement had been shattered by a passionate affair between Edward Angove and his brother's wife.

Who was right? Should she make some effort to find out whether the tale was a figment of the older woman's imagination? She hoped that her uncertainty wasn't showing in her face.

'Before you make a final decision,' Philip said uncompromisingly, 'I think you should at least meet the person that decision is going to affect most. I want you to come to Motupipi with me this afternoon to meet my mother.'

Antonia sent him a startled look. His intent gaze and compressed, merciless mouth, the forceful determination that set his face into an autocratic mask, almost swayed her into agreeing meekly.

Just in time common sense pulled her back from the brink. Her eyes, caught by the emerald spell of his, wavered as she drew in a deep breath and firmed the clean-cut bow of her mouth into a straight line, every bit as obstinate as his.

'I can't do that,' she objected, frowning when she saw the glitter fade from his eyes to be replaced by a steely impassivity.

There was much more to this man than sexual charisma and casual, confident social success, the smooth polish of his moneyed background. He possessed a concentrated authority that came from within, based on a character that was formidable and ruthless. A chill worked its way up her spine as she realised that he was truly dangerous. Damn Heather, with her feudal ideas of loyalty!

CHAPTER TWO

'WHY?' The word was a whiplash.

Harried, Antonia cast a time-wasting glance around the room, but the remorseless insistence of his tone and expression was a summons she couldn't disobey. 'Well, to start off with, if she's ill my arrival on the scene is only going to upset her more.'

'She's not ill. She's just delicate. And of course I won't tell her who you are.'

'I don't want to go there under false pretences,' she said, and could have died of embarrassment.

He laughed. A sudden curl of attraction twisted into life in the pit of Antonia's stomach.

'It won't be under false pretences. I shall introduce you as a friend.' Quite deliberately he let his eyes rest on her face in a sensuous appraisal that pulled her skin tight. 'I think we could be friends, you and I.'

Flakes of colour heated Antonia's cheeks. Very crisply she said, 'Look, if your mother is so upset by the tape, I can put a restriction on it for, say, twenty years.'

He considered this, his eyes never leaving her face. 'I'll certainly suggest that to her, but I still think you should meet her.'

'I can't let myself be swayed by sentiment,' she said, endeavouring for a tone of blunt matter-of-fact formality, but only managing, she suspected, to produce a defensive whine.

'Surely the very concept of an oral history unit is based on sentiment,' he returned.

'No!' Stung, she pointed her chin at him, stating emphatically, 'It's as valid a repository as any archive.'

His smile was a masterpiece of contempt. 'Even if there are lies——?'

25

She leaned forward. 'If you think that every word written in the past and used today in the study of history is the truth, then you're far more naïve than your appearance and behaviour lead me to believe,' she flashed back.

Unexpectedly, he grinned, and that dimple made a fleeting appearance. Dragging her gaze away, Antonia realised that she could get used to looking for it.

'*Touché.*' His voice softened, became lazy, dangerously coaxing. 'Look, why don't you come up with me this afternoon? I can guarantee a pleasant afternoon.' He paused before adding, 'If you do, I'll back off.'

Antonia stared at him suspiciously, but, although he resembled nothing so much as a lean, powerful, entirely ruthless corsair, the only emotion revealed in his angular features was an arrogant determination that she do as he willed.

Almost unconsciously she relaxed. Of course he was planning to manipulate her, to play on her sympathies, but what harm could that do? Plenty of other men had tried, and failed.

She was confident of her ability to withstand Philip Angove as well. But why make a battle of it? If that was what it took to get him off her back, why not go up to his feudal estate and meet his delicate mother, and get it over and done with?

Both of them understood that he had the power and the influence to make her life so difficult at the unit that she would eventually have to hand in her resignation. He had offered her a way out, and, even though it was insulting to be considered so easily influenced, she was accustomed to it by now.

She could deal with him—she had grown strong enough to deal with anything—but it would be easier if she accepted the olive-branch he was handing out. Always provided Philip Angove kept his word, of course.

She sneaked a swift glance at his face. Carved in clean lines, it registered an inflexible will that somehow convinced her she could trust him. It would not fit in with his self-image, she thought shrewdly, to go back on his word.

Anyway, it was worth a shot, and he would soon learn that she was impervious to any pressure.

'All right,' she said, carefully keeping any sign of ca pitulation from her voice and expression. 'I'll come to meet your mother. But not today—I have an interview this afternoon, and the rest of the week is fully booked, too. I'll drive up on Saturday.'

He was an expert negotiator. Not a sign of triumph appeared in his expression. Instead he smiled, and Antonia warmed involuntarily at the smoky appreciation in his eyes. He had the fierce, honed features of a predator, but the sensualist prowled not far beneath the surface.

Careful, she whispered to herself.

'Fine,' he said. 'I'll look forward to it.'

And that was that. He made no effort to hurry her along, but spent the rest of the lunch-hour talking. He didn't flirt, but his eyes lingered on Antonia's face and mouth, and beneath his knowledgeable, perceptive conversation there ran the flattering, hidden river of masculine awareness.

But it was his conversation that fascinated her. He possessed a well read man's ability to discuss almost any subject intelligently, as well as a cold incisiveness that sliced through to the heart of an argument.

Accustomed to men who refused to look past her face to the woman inside, Antonia found his attitude amazingly seductive. In only a few minutes she had dropped her guard sufficiently to ignore the warning signals her instincts sent her, responding with an animation that would have surprised most of the men she had been out with.

He drove her back to the museum, where he insisted on escorting her to the office door. 'We'll expect you around eleven on Saturday, shall we?' he said, smiling down at her. 'You can stay to lunch and have a look around, then get home in plenty of time before it gets dark.'

Compulsively her eyes searched for the dimple, but this time it didn't appear. 'Yes, that sounds fine,' she replied, a tiny shiver whispering through her nerves as she met his eyes. They were so green, with those golden flames at the heart. They seemed to see right into her, to the hidden part of herself that nobody, except perhaps her oldest friend, had ever discerned.

But once in the office, free of his potent physical presence, some of her hard-won caution came surging back. Of course he couldn't see past her defences. That searching stare was just one of the arsenal of weapons he employed, and very effective it was, too. It made the recipient feel that she was the only woman he had ever noticed. No doubt he used it to excellent effect in his love life.

Quelling an odd little pang, she turned to face her assistant.

'How did things go?' Heather asked tentatively.

Antonia disliked rebuking anyone, but experience had taught her that sometimes it was a necessity that couldn't be avoided. 'I think we'd better have a talk about your part in this fiasco,' she said firmly.

The talk ended with Heather in tears, but insisting nevertheless that she would do the exact same thing if the situation ever arose again. 'They've been so kind to us,' she whimpered. 'When Dad was sick and off work for nine months they paid his wages and didn't put us out of the house, and it's not many farmers who would have done that, believe me.'

Possibly, Antonia thought cynically, because not many farmers were as rich as the Angoves.

'Mrs Angove is a darling,' Heather went on defiantly, 'and a real *lady*. Nobody should have to put up with foul, nasty-minded gossip like that. I'm sorry, Antonia, but I had to tell them.'

'Then perhaps,' Antonia said in her quietest voice, 'you'd better consider whether you are suited to this sort of work. I can understand, even admire, your loyalty to the Angoves, but there is such a thing as loyalty to your occupation, and you didn't show much of that, did you? I can't see myself ever trusting you fully again.'

Heather stared at her. It was clear that this was not a reaction she had expected. 'You don't really mean that, do you?' she asked uncertainly.

'Yes, I do.'

'But—Philip wants me to work here.'

'As a spy?'

'No!'

The younger woman looked at her with such a wounded expression that Antonia felt a pang of compassion. This was a difficult decision for Heather to make, but she had to face the implications of her actions.

'I'm sorry,' Antonia said evenly, 'but you can't have it both ways. Either you're loyal to the unit, or you're loyal to the Angoves. They're a well known family, they could easily turn up in other tapes, and I don't want to have to watch you to make sure you don't run off to tell them what others have said about them, or edit out everything that is even mildly censorious.'

'I wouldn't——' Heather was shocked.

Antonia silenced her with a steady look. 'How do I know that?' she asked. 'No, don't say anything more now. Think about it during the week, and tell me next Monday morning where your greater loyalty lies. We'll take it from there.'

Leaving a considerably chastened assistant behind her, she went off to the preliminary interview, trying to squelch a forbidden excitement that was due to the prospect of seeing Philip Angove again.

That night in her small town house she found it hard to get to sleep. In the end she was reduced to switching on the light and reading. But when she closed her eyes the olive-skinned, hawk-nosed face of Philip Angove

appeared once more, smiling with his effortless, enigmatic, frightening charm. He even turned up in her
dreams.

She managed to banish him from her mind during the
rest of that busy, hot week, but on Friday night, at the
elegant apartment which Tiffany and Eliot Buchanan
used when they had to stay in Auckland, she said idly,
'I'm going up to Motupipi tomorrow.'

On the first day of primary school Tiffany Brandon
and Antonia Ridd had vowed to be best friends forever.
Unlike most such vows, this one had never been broken.
Now Tiffany directed a sharp look at her. 'Philip
Angove's place?'

'Is there another one?'

'Don't be smart!' Tiffany grinned. 'Come on, Tonia,
spill it out. Why are you going to Motupipi?'

'He wants to charm me into erasing a tape. I can't tell
you any more than that.'

'In that case,' Tiffany observed drily, 'it will be erased.
The man has infinite charm.'

'Like Bryan.'

'Not in the least like Beastly Bryan Howard. All he
had was good looks and the kind of arrogant young
man's confidence we all took for sophistication because
we were too young and naïve to know the real thing.
Philip's a true sophisticate.'

'Do you like him?'

Black eyes gleaming, Tiffany laughed. 'Philip? Of
course I like him. He's a gorgeous man. If I weren't still
wildly in love with Eliot I'd probably be joining the queue
of hopeful young women intent on catching Philip's eye.
I gather you liked him, too.'

'Hmm, he was very—charming.' Antonia knew she
was being evasive. Tiffany knew it, too. To wipe the grin
off her face Antonia finished, 'Though there were several
minutes when he looked far more fierce than persuasive.'

'He's rather feared in the business world. Eliot says
he's as tough as leather, but scrupulously honest.'

A bit like Eliot, in fact. Idly, as though the question had no significance, Antonia asked, 'What's his mother like?'

Tiffany's alert dark eyes softened. 'She's a lovely woman. So kind, and infinitely thoughtful. She's a great friend of Eliot's mother, and I'm sure that they got together to ease my transition into Eliot's world. Mrs Angove introduced me to everyone, and she—well, I suppose she gave me confidence, and when people saw that she accepted me they did, too. It's a pity they don't entertain much any more. Her health's not too good— a blood condition, I believe. She's not really sick, but just has to take care.'

Antonia nodded, and turned her head to look out of the window. The Buchanans' apartment was on the top floor so it had a magnificent view over the harbour, sprinkled now with yachts whose owners had taken an early start to the weekend. Their sails, brilliantly coloured, were like small, vivid butterflies on the water.

'Philip's been seeing quite a bit of Laurie Preece,' Tiffany went on. 'I believe his mother is very keen for them to marry, and Laurie herself is quite sure it's going to come off. It would be a good thing for both families; Laurie's father is on the look-out for a son to take over the business. Not that the Angoves need the money, but the family has a history of marrying well. Philip isn't giving anything away, though. He still appears with other women from time to time.'

Laurie Preece was a model; her exquisite face and slender body adorned magazines all over the South Pacific. Something so fragile that she wasn't even aware of its existence shattered deep inside Antonia. Stupid to feel that just because she had reacted so swiftly, so blatantly, to Philip he would feel the same. A man who could marry a beautiful woman like Laurie Preece wouldn't find anything at all attractive in ordinary Antonia Ridd.

'He has that air,' she said. 'Patrician as hell.'

'Ah, that's the aristocratic background. The first Angove to settle in New Zealand was the second son of an earl!'

Antonia sent her a lazy grin, but refused to react to her teasing.

Giving up, Tiffany resumed, 'The Angoves are really old money. They know everybody. You meet the most intriguing people at Motupipi—politicians, opera stars, titled relatives, polo players, best-selling writers. All buttressed by a solid weight of New Zealand society. They used to hold huge, wonderful parties, with caterers up from town and people flying in from overseas. There was a story going around a few years back about bribes actually being offered by one particular person to several hostesses who might be able to get him in by the back door, so to speak.'

'They move in elevated circles,' Antonia murmured drily.

Tiffany gave a lurking grin. 'Actually, I think you could say that the Angoves are the elevated circle people like Bryan Howard aspire to!'

'This is New Zealand,' Antonia objected. 'We don't go in for that sort of snobbery.'

'Some people do. And the Angoves really are different. For years all the Angove daughters went to France to finishing-schools; some came back, but quite a few married overseas, so Philip's connected to some very interesting people all around the world. One of his cousins lives in a magnificent plantation house with white pillars somewhere in the deep south.' She drawled the final words in a mock American accent.

'Finishing-schools! I really *hate* that sort of pretension. That's what the pioneers came out here to avoid!'

Tiffany laughed. 'Yes, but the Angoves came too, so the pioneers dipped out! Don't go taking a scunner to the man, for heaven's sake, just because he's rich and confident. The Angoves are not snobs; I liked them both very much. They're not like the Howards at all. Anyway, what does it matter? Eliot grew up in a family with loads of cash, he's tough and opinionated and arrogant, and you like *him*.'

Whenever Eliot looked at Tiffany, it was as though to him she was the most rare and precious thing in the universe. Antonia smiled. 'Eliot is different.'

'Not that different,' his loving wife of five years said drily. 'The arrogant male isn't very far beneath the surface, believe me. You just haven't seen it often. You know what your problem is, don't you? You've never really got over what Bloody Bryan Howard and his harridan of a mother did to you. They made you believe you were inferior, and somehow, in spite of the master's degree with honours, and the success you've made of your life, and the fact that you have friends galore, you still *feel* inferior, as though the only thing men want from you is what Bryan did—to take you to bed. You look at every man you meet with that sort of bleak caution, and you freeze them off before they've had a chance to prove they're nothing like Bryan.'

'Rubbish,' Antonia said crisply.

'If it's rubbish, why aren't you married? You're really attractive, you have such a lot to give a man, and yet you won't let any of them get close enough to find out about it!'

'You saw Eliot before I did, and he's the only man I like well enough to marry,' Antonia said lightly, smiling.

Tiffany snorted. '*Like*? Liking's not enough, you dope. You need passion and respect as well as liking. I worry about you, Tonia.'

Antonia said obstinately, 'I've tried passion once and I didn't like what it did to my thought processes. I'll give it a miss, thanks very much.'

'That's the point, though. It's a necessary, even a vital part of love and marriage. You're still fixated on wretched Bryan——'

'I am not!'

'Yes, you are. Oh, I don't mean you want him, but he's still ruling your life. Tonia, you have to extract what benefit you can from your experiences and then put them behind you.'

'That's exactly what I have done. I'm not going to let myself be carried away by hormones and sex ever again.' Antonia did her best to conceal the stiffly defensive note in her voice, but Tiffany knew her too well.

'You feel too much, too deeply,' she said sympathetically. 'That's why Bryan was able to hurt you so badly. So you built yourself these defences, just in case it happened again. But you have to gamble to win.'

'And if you lose?'

'You pick yourself up and gamble some more. OK, OK, I won't say any more. At least, not after you tell me why, unlike every other woman who realises that Philip Angove is unattached, you're not going to at least make some tiny attempt to catch his eye.'

A shivery little *frisson* brushed across Antonia's nerves. 'Because I thought he was arrogant and macho and overbearing.'

'Clearly he impressed you no end.' Tiffany grinned wickedly. 'That's exactly what I thought Eliot was when I first met him. Dangerous!'

Antonia believed her. Eliot Buchanan was not the sort of man she would have expected her friend to fall in love with, yet their marriage was extremely happy. Antonia sometimes had to stifle a pang of aching envy when she saw the way they smiled at each other.

'Well, it's a pity,' Tiffany sighed, 'but Philip Angove is probably not the sort of man you could ever bring yourself to trust, even though he's really nothing like Bryan Howard. However, if you want a nice, gentle man, you should at least give one a chance when he comes along.'

Back at home, Antonia found herself too strung up to go to bed. In the end she worked for an hour or so in her garden by the light of a brilliant harvest moon, mulling over Tiffany's forthright words. Surely it wasn't stupid to hold out for something more than the wild desire that had got her into so much trouble nine years ago?

Was Tiffany right? Did she send out signals saying 'Keep Off'? She sat back on her heels and surveyed a particularly enthusiastic runner of twitch grass. But how did you reverse signals—and did she particularly want to? She had made herself a very comfortable life, with good friends, a job she enjoyed; she was content. Why be tempted to throw it all away because a man's virile, honed masculinity tugged at her senses?

Frowning, she got to her feet. The whole question was academic, anyway; Philip Angove had seemed to feel that flashpoint of attraction too, but that didn't mean he was going to do anything about it. And if Tiffany was right and he was going to marry the model, then Antonia Ridd didn't need to worry any further!

Unless, of course, he had Bryan's attitude to these things. Bryan hadn't wanted Antonia for a wife; he planned to marry another woman, a *suitable* woman, but he'd seen no reason why highly unsuitable Antonia, daughter of a woman who'd become notorious in the district, shouldn't be his mistress.

The rejection and bitterness still ate like acid into her soul. Standing with trowel in hand, she looked around at the beautiful garden she had made for herself. It was her favourite hobby, one she had had since childhood, and that, along with her friendship with Tiffany and her deep-seated need to prove herself, had been what kept her sane after Bryan's betrayal had thrown her life into shambles.

One day she planned to own enough land to really let herself go with designing the perfect garden. It would, she thought with a wry, cynical smile as she went in-doors, give her far more pleasure than any man ever had.

Waking the next morning to an exquisite summer's day, she firmly refused to acknowledge the needle of tension that probed her nerves. But the sly anticipation continued to prickle while she finished her usual Saturday morning chores, increasing in intensity when she drove through the wide-ranging suburbs and along the north-western motorway, through the tiny town of Helensville on its mangrove-infested river, and on beside the huge and magnificent Kaipara Harbour. It had, she knew, the world's longest harbour coastline, but she couldn't see much of it from the road, although she stopped at one or two look-out points, more to put off the inevitable meeting with Philip Angove than to appreciate the view.

Such procrastination was foreign to her. It had taken her half an hour to decide what to wear! Antonia despised herself; the last time she had dithered so uselessly about clothes was when she had been eighteen and thought she was in love.

She despised herself even more for choosing a sleek ice-blue dress in a crisp cotton instead of the trousers and silk shirt she had originally intended to wear.

Just because your legs are short, she snorted as the small car crested a hill. Well, not exactly short—they were actually in proportion with her figure, but compared to...oh, admit it, compared to Laurie Preece's legs, which went on for ever, her own were definitely lacking in length.

Firmly setting her mind to other things, like the appearance that morning of a bud on her Bridal Bouquet lily, Antonia drove steadily northwards.

Just where Philip had said it would be, the turn-off to the station appeared on the left-hand of the road. 'Motupipi Station', a sign said in bold letters, and beneath it was the name 'P.E. Angove'. Something ominously close to a butterfly brushed wings against the sides of Antonia's stomach.

Telling herself sternly not to be so stupid—she was immune to that dark, predator's attraction—Antonia turned her aged car in between the two huge flame trees that marked the entrance, and continued down the drive.

Philip hadn't thought to mention that the homestead was nowhere in sight from the road. The drive stretched across rolling farmlands, heading directly towards the glittering water of the harbour.

Of course Motupipi had been settled before any roads existed, so all the main buildings would be on the coast, within reach of the small ships the pioneers had relied on for transport.

Antonia glanced around as she drove onwards. She had expected to see paddocks crisped by drought, but Motupipi had definitely had more rain over the summer than Auckland. Although the grass was not exactly lush there was still plenty of feed for the animals in the paddocks. The sign of a good farmer, she thought knowledgeably.

Her eyes lingered on huge, pale Maine Anjou cattle, then moved to the more common Angus, gleaming black in the late summer sun as they lifted their heads to stare at her.

At last, just as she was beginning to wonder whether she was ever going to get there, the road crested a hill and there was the heart of the station, a cluster of houses set along a beach. Behind them a wide, neatly fenced valley ran back towards the highway.

At the top of the hill the road divided, one fork leading down to the settlement on the beach, the other diving across the brow and off to the right. Firmly controlling the butterflies, now a small flock, that lurched uncomfortably about in her stomach, Antonia drove sedately down towards the bay, a champagne crescent of sand anchored at one end by a long jetty on wooden piles. The valley behind the houses was punctuated by a vast woolshed and a complex of sheep and cattleyards and other sheds of various sorts, sheltered by the dark bulk of macrocarpa hedges.

No one house seemed to be set apart a little, as surely the owner's would be? Biting her bottom lip, Antonia stopped and climbed out of the car, looking about her for some clue to the whereabouts of the homestead.

Silence, broken only by the stridulation of cicadas, lay in a lovely blanket over land and sea, its benediction soothing her into something approaching her normal serenity. Her mouth, that ridiculous cupid's bow, curled up in a smile. Motupipi was lovely.

Her eyes roamed the scene before her. A light breeze ruffled the waters of the Kaipara, gleaming blue and silver under the benign sun. Breathing deeply of the clean, sparkling air, crisp with the first faint intimations of autumn yet still warm, Antonia's spirits rose.

The smile vanished when she heard a man's voice coming from the stockyards. It was deep and dark and soft, so that the words were impossible to make out, but even at this distance Antonia recognised Philip's voice, the way its textured darkness shaded into undertones of sensuality.

Something unknown whispered across her nerves. After a frozen moment she commanded herself to stop acting like an idiot, and go and tell him she had arrived. Halfway across the cropped grass to the stockpens she heard him again, soothing, teasing, a note of humour shading the words, but always crooning in a slurred, shaman's whisper that touched some buried awareness within her.

A horse, she realised, shaken by peculiar relief, of course, he's gentling a horse! Narrowing her eyes against the brilliant light from the sea and sky, she could make them out behind the rails, catch the slow, unhurried stroking of a lean hand across the horse's glossy chestnut shoulder. When he straightened Antonia drew in a shaking, startled breath. But he hadn't seen her; his attention was concentrated wholly on the horse.

A strange compulsion held her still, motionless as an animal eyed by a snake. Her heart thudded loudly in her ears, drowning out the persistent drone of the cicadas. With dilated eyes she followed the smooth, oddly compelling movements of the man behind the railings, noting the poised, watchful stance, the sheen of sweat on flexing muscles, the gleaming, obsidian hair.

He was as supple as a great cat, she thought reluctantly, with a balanced, feline grace, a linked harmony of muscle and sinew and strength that revealed perfect health and a deep, physical confidence in himself. That same in-built assurance and poise had made him stand out in the sophisticated environs of the restaurant.

There was a sudden blur of action as he swung himself on to the back of the horse. Antonia sucked in a swift breath. Time stood still until the horse's head went down between its legs, its back arched, and it bucked, letting out a shriek of such defiance that Antonia's blood iced over. Her pulse sped up unbearably, deafening her as she ran across to the high, timber rails around the yard, and peered between them.

The horse was striving with single-minded determination to get rid of the man on its back, its strong haunches quivering with effort as it bucked and plunged and fought, screaming in a mixture of anger and betrayal and frustration.

But the man was its master. No matter how cunningly the horse twisted and kicked the rider stayed in the saddle, his lean, tanned hands confident on the reins, the muscles in his thighs and calves clamped around the chestnut barrel of the horse, holding himself there by skill and strength and a horse-wizard's intuition that warned him what the animal was going to do next.

Sensation as sharp and keen as a lance pierced Antonia. Hands gripping the sun-warmed timber, she watched, awed and impressed and thrilled by the raw contest of will and power and determination. Even though she realised that Philip Angove was helped by the fact that the horse had no real vice in him, some buried, primitive part of her revelled in the sight of the man taming the beast.

'Excuse me, miss.' The voice from behind was not exactly welcoming.

Dragged out of her complete absorption, Antonia swung around guiltily. The man watching her was tall and middle-aged, with a fair-skinned face carved by sun and weather.

'Are you looking for someone?' he asked, frowning, his eyes narrowing as they came to rest on her face.

Antonia's tone was forced. 'Yes. I—that is——'

Suspicion deepened in his expression. Pulling herself together, she finished, 'I have an appointment to meet Philip Angove at eleven.' She essayed a smile. 'I saw he was busy, so I thought I'd wait.'

A muffled sound from the horse whipped both heads around. The animal flung itself on to the ground, but Antonia's horror was rapidly replaced by astonishment as she realised that Philip had anticipated just such a trick. Agile as a cat, he stepped off, waited half crouching for the animal to realise he was no longer there, then as it clambered up swung back into the saddle. Antonia's breath caught in her throat. He was more than good, he was superb! And he was laughing, the lean, striking face creased with a keen, atavistic delight in the age-old contest of skill and stamina and intelligence.

'He's got Sultan's measure well and truly,' the newcomer said, nodding. His voice was husky, a little rough, as though he had just woken up. 'He should be ready for you in a few minutes, unless you'd like to go on to the homestead and wait for him there?'

Feeling a complete fool, Antonia gave him her best oral historian's smile, professional and competent. For heaven's sake, to be caught drooling over a man on a horse like a flibbertigibbet teenager in love with romance! 'No, I'll wait here, thanks.'

But the horse had done its dash. Philip's voice, slow and soft and sensuous as he urged it towards the railing, was producing the desired result.

Only after it had obeyed him by taking him several times around the yards did he swing off and remove the saddle and bridle, his voice flowed smoothly over the animal, his hand stroked along the sweat-streaked neck. Whickering, the animal thrust its nose into his chest, and Philip laughed, dark magic in his tone, and produced something from his pocket.

It was then that he saw Antonia. Just for a moment his eyes raked her with the same kind of fierce possessiveness that he'd shown towards the animal he had broken to his touch, and an answering flare of excitement irradiated her soul. He smiled.

A sharp jolt of shockingly sweet sensation stabbed through her. In spite of the heat she felt colour drain from her skin. Philip Angove was altogether too attractive for her peace of mind—how fortunate that after today she need never see him again!

Still hot and prickly, she summoned a smile in answer to his. 'Thanks for looking after Antonia, Mike,' he said easily. 'Antonia, this is Mike Reynolds, who manages Motupipi. Mike, I'm sure you've heard of Antonia from Heather.'

Mike Reynolds was, of course, Heather's father, the man who had taken Heather's disloyalty to her work for granted, the man who had carried the knowledge of Elva Collins's tape to Philip.

Antonia looked challengingly at him as she shook hands; he seemed a little taken aback, but although his curiosity was palpable he merely nodded in greeting. 'Yes, of course. Philip, you'll want to talk to Miss Ridd, so I'll rub Sultan down.'

Antonia barely heard Philip's answer, registering the tone of voice more than the words; the smoky sensuality he had used on the horse had been replaced by a crisp authority that was infinitely less wearing on Antonia's nerves.

'Are you sure you should be up?' he said. 'How's the tonsillitis?'

Heather's father shrugged. 'Better.'

Philip shot him a keen glance but said nothing more about it, continuing with a few succinct observations about the beef herd.

'Right,' he said finally, when Mike Reynolds, after another nod at Antonia, strode off towards a tractor, 'I've got the Land Rover. If you go ahead you won't eat my dust. The drive forks about five hundred metres back the way you came; turn left and keep going until you reach the homestead. It's another kilometre on.'

Mutely Antonia nodded, climbing into her small, hot car with a speed he probably construed as a retreat. He wouldn't be far wrong at that, she thought wearily.

The homestead, which she had assumed would be an old Victorian house, was a magnificent modern building facing across a green slope of gardens to a pale slice of beach. Out in the bay slept a tiny tree-covered island, remote with the mystery that all islands wore like a cloak; it must, she realised, be the Motupipi the station was named after. Straight behind it was the entrance to the harbour, the cliffs on either side of the gap connected by the white waters of the bar.

The view was breathtaking, but it was the homestead that made Antonia gasp with delight.

Pale ochre, a lighter shade than the earth in the roadside cuttings, the huge, low house blended into the landscape. The roof was supported by great round columns of the same ochre render as the rest of the house. They, and the palms that waved about the building, combined with the architectural planting of the several acres of gardens to give the place an air of serenity and strength.

Looking around with the eye of a keen and knowledgeable gardener, Antonia realised that whoever had designed the well groomed grounds had provided a magnificent setting for the house, but that was all. Her fingers itched to soften the framework of trees and shrubs with flowers and gardens, to provide the grounds with the same atmosphere of mystery and serenity as the house.

The car slid to a halt on the pebbled courtyard outside two enormous carved front doors, their monumental qualities emphasised by the lacy fronds of tree ferns. But what was needed to set off the simple structural forms were cheeky, simple, jewel-coloured impatiens flowers beneath them.

Antonia drew a deep breath and got out. It was absolutely silent, as though she had somehow walked through a chink in the universe and was on some distant planet, some magic place where the rules of everyday life did not hold.

Every cell in her body quivering with stupid, unfounded apprehension, she swallowed, then walked up the wide, shallow steps into the shade of the portico. It took an effort of will to stand still and wait as the Land Rover came closer and closer.

By the time the noise of the engine had died in the heated air she had managed to regain a little composure, but even so her eyes dilated as Philip got out and came towards her, the sun striking sable fire from the black waves of his hair. The evocative scent of the horse he had been riding mingled with the faint, far from unpleasant aroma of active male, disturbing, upsettingly stimulating.

'The door's open,' he said as he swung one side back. 'Welcome to Motupipi.'

His smile held the tinge of mockery, as though he sensed her wide-eyed awe, and was amused by it. Antonia's chin came up. Walking precisely, she moved past him into the house.

CHAPTER THREE

THE big hall was lit by windows that opened out on to the harbour. As far as the eye could see there was nothing but that incredible silvery blue harbour framed by the positive, intense green curves of the land. Acutely aware of the man who walked silently beside her, Antonia cast a respectful glance at a magnificent grandfather clock. Eighteenth century, possibly copied from a plate in Chippendale's *Director*. If this one was as genuine as the one in the museum it was worth hundreds of thousands of dollars.

On the wall was a Monet. One of the poppies-in-a-field Monets, and, she thought with an odd terrified skip of her heart, not the worst she had seen by any means. Just who were the Angoves, who had pictures like this on their walls?

They were approaching a corner when a door a little further along opened, and a pleasant-faced woman in her late thirties or early forties, girded in an apron that meant business, came through. Her face broke into a smile—did anyone ever frown at him? Antonia wondered crossly—as she said, 'Oh, there you are! Philip, your mother is getting impatient!'

'We won't be a moment,' he said calmly. 'Antonia, this is Brenda Green. Brenda runs the homestead and Motupipi with an iron hand, but she makes the best muffins north of Auckland so we let her get away with murder.'

Brenda laughed. 'Which means,' she said to Antonia, giving her a shrewd glance, 'that he wants me to make tea.'

'We'll have it in my mother's sitting-room.'

So she was to be introduced to Mrs Angove immediately—no doubt so that she could begin to appreciate the older woman's charm and sterling character.

Philip continued on down the hall with a noiseless economy of effort that intimidated her anew. Although she was slender and possessed her fair share of grace, she felt clumsy beside his lean form, and as though in some subtle, complex way she was being threatened.

His mother waited for them in her sitting-room, both exquisitely decorated, Antonia thought irreverently as she was introduced. It didn't seem possible that this thin, still beautiful woman in her mid-sixties had ever given rise to such gossip.

Moira Angove smiled as she greeted her; that smile was radiance personified, yet gentle, almost serene, with it.

Five minutes later Antonia was admitting that Tiffany had been right; Mrs Angove was a darling. Like everyone else she had fallen under the woman's spell.

'But how lovely you are! You remind me of my favourite aunt!' Philip's mother said.

'She was a flapper in the Roaring Twenties, I suppose.' Antonia qualified her sigh with a smile.

'She was an absolute pet,' her hostess said warmly, adding, 'Do sit down. Did you have a good drive up?'

'Yes, thank you. I didn't realise how few cars there are on this road.'

'It's because it's not sealed over Cleesby's Hill, just before Wellsford.'

After a few more pleasantries Philip said, 'If you'll both excuse me, I'll remove the horse smell.' He gave Antonia a swift smile. 'I'll be back shortly.'

Mrs Angove waited until he was out of the room before saying, 'My husband was one of the old school, with rigid ideas about what is done and what isn't. Smelling of horse inside the house just wasn't on! He found the modern trend towards informality very difficult to cope with. Philip follows him, but isn't quite so inflexible.

One can get too hung up on the letter of the law, can't one, and forget that courtesy should come from the heart?'

The housekeeper arrived with the tea. Then, with cup and saucer in her hand and a slice of buttery shortbread to eat, Antonia admired her hostess's sitting-room.

'Why, thank you.' Clearly, Moira Angove was delighted. She told Antonia how the redecoration of the room had been a surprise for her when she came home from a stay in hospital.

'Of course Philip didn't do it himself, he's much too busy, but he's rather good at cracking a whip, and it was finished in about three weeks, which is truly amazing.'

Not if you had money! But such was the indefinable charm of the woman that it was just a passing thought. Antonia began to relax, although she was still very aware of any sound outside which might signify the return of the man who owned all this.

Clearly the Angove family was seriously rich. Antonia began to have some awareness of how Elva Collins's insistence on having her story heard could affect them, especially the woman in the chair opposite. Moira Angove's thin hands trembled when she poured out the tea so that the magnificent diamonds in her engagement ring scintillated in the bright light.

Oh, Philip Angove was very astute! How had he known that she would be moved unbearably by the gallant, erect little figure? Yet Antonia knew that she could not let her sympathy overwhelm her.

Mrs Angove broke into her harried thoughts. 'Tegan Jones did the actual design, and found a few bits and pieces to set it off properly. She's absolutely brilliant, I think, don't you? Laurie helped her, which was charming of her, and rather touching, because this is not her style of thing at all. Do have some more shortbread, my dear. Brenda is famous for her shortbread. A completely modern woman, is Laurie. Do you know her? Laurie Preece?'

'No, I don't. Of course I've seen her photos in the magazines. She's beautiful.'

'Lovely. And very up-to-date, which is why I was somewhat surprised when she helped with this, because one thing I am not is modern.' She looked around her with a comical expression which made Antonia smile. 'I don't think she actually *did* anything, you know, but she has exquisite taste, just like her mother, who is one of my dearest friends. It was kind of her to interest herself in the project.'

Was her hostess warning her about the beauteous Laurie's place in Philip's life? Quite possibly. Kindly, of course; it wasn't possible to see Mrs Angove as anything other than kind.

Antonia was refusing a second cup of tea when Philip came back, lean and lethal in a pair of casual grey trousers and a short-sleeved cotton shirt several shades paler that emphasised those astounding green-gold eyes. Mrs Angove smiled sunnily as he came in through the door, and said something, but Antonia couldn't make out the words, for his appearance hit her like a bombshell.

Of course the effect he had on her was purely physical, but why? He wasn't handsome; she almost laughed aloud at the thought. Philip Angove transcended handsomeness. It was not the boldly compelling lines of his face that caused the searing rush of attraction she was trying so desperately to hide.

Antonia's breath caught in a knot in her chest. The wildfire magic had been called into being by her first glimpse of his black hair and broad shoulders and the narrow line of waist and hips and thighs, the lithe animal grace of his movements. Philip's magnetism had wakened something buried deep inside, something unknown and primitive. The arrogantly chiselled face merely bound her more securely in the elemental chains of attraction.

It had started as soon as she saw him, but what had made it impossible to overcome was the sound of his voice, soft and dark and sensuous as he had gentled the horse. Was that how he would sound when he made love?

She was mad. She despised men who thought their name and money gave them rights above those of lesser mortals. God, hadn't she had enough experience of them, the presumptuous, selfish ones who abused their power and position?

They paraded before her in a warning procession. First her father, who had left her mother almost destitute, then Bryan Howard. After him there had been the lecturer who'd hinted that her grades would be much better if she went to bed with him. Each rejection, each misuse of power, had left a scar on her soul that was only slowly healing.

Yet somehow she could not fit Philip into that rogues' gallery. He was—different.

And you are a mermaid, she thought cynically.

Until the moment his fingers had closed on her arm she hadn't known that passion could scorch like a whip, searing through common sense and indignation and mistrust. Her weakness, the helpless treachery of her body, terrified her. Even with Bryan it had not been like this, and she had come out of that episode with her self-respect in shreds.

'So I thought you might like to come down to the beach for a swim after lunch,' Philip said. 'Antonia?'

She swallowed, forcing her mind to take in what he was saying. 'I'm not a terribly good swimmer,' she improvised lamely.

'No?' The emerald flick of his glance revealed that he didn't believe her. He drawled, 'That's a pity. We could go riding, then. There are some magnificent views from the hills.'

Antonia lifted her head, meeting with what she hoped was dignity and self-possession a look in which challenge was spiced with mockery. 'I'm afraid I don't ride.'

'Then we'll take the Land Rover.' His smile didn't soften Philip's controlled mouth.

Waiting in vain for the dimple, she said, 'All right.'

So after an excellent lunch Antonia allowed herself to be put into the Land Rover. If the whole object of this exercise was to make her feel sympathy for Mrs Angove, or to convince her that there was no way the woman could have indulged in an affair with her husband's brother, those aims were already achieved.

Perhaps Philip had seen that; it could explain why they were driving along the top of a steep gully instead of sitting down in that fabulous house where she could continue to be charmed by his mother.

Of course Philip Angove had been well brought up, she thought with a faint touch of malice, which meant that one must entertain one's guests, treat them with courtesy if not respect. Just like Bryan, who had stripped her self-esteem from her without once raising his voice. Money and social position mightn't do much for your character, but it helped your manners no end.

'That,' came Philip's calm, judicious voice from beside her, 'is an odd expression. Is the track making you nervous?'

'No, not in the least.' She had driven around enough farm tracks in her youth to no longer wonder why they invariably skirted the steepest, barest drops on the property.

'My driving, perhaps?'

She smiled ironically. 'Your driving, as I'm sure you know, is superb. Oh!'

He had turned the Land Rover on to a small flat area and now brought it to a halt so that she could see the panorama in front of them. 'Oh,' she repeated softly, 'this is beautiful!'

The harbour spread below like a smooth gleaming slab of mother-of-pearl. The strange humpy formations that were stabilised sandhills made two thin barriers between the harbour and the wide, dangerous Tasman Sea. Today the waves were gentle over the killer bar which had caused so many shipwrecks, so many deaths. The combers would be curling quietly up the unprotected beaches on the seaward side of each peninsula, foaming over the dark sand like white lace against sombre crêpe. Antonia's gaze lingered, finding an obscure source of strength in the serene sweep of sea, the timeless shapes of the hills and valleys.

'Have you told your mother about the twenty-year restriction?' she asked abruptly.

'Yes. It's not good enough.'

She hadn't known until then just how much she wanted Mrs Angove to agree. A flash of sheer anger at the older woman's intransigence shook her. 'I'm afraid that's all I can do,' she said, trying not to sound stubborn.

'It's not enough. I want that tape erased, or at the very least edited.'

'Censored, you mean.'

He directed a sharp, hard look at her. 'Would that be so bad?'

She stared obstinately out the window. 'Yes. And certainly contrary to the terms of your uncle's trust.'

He made no answer, but Antonia didn't fool herself into thinking that was an end to the matter. She continued staring through the windscreen, and after a while began once more to take in what she was looking at.

The landscape was as varied and beautiful as any in New Zealand. Sleek, slow-moving cattle grazed placidly in paddocks on flat reclaimed land fringed by olive-green mangroves. Further inland hills rose, some blue with bush, some starkly green where the pioneers had felled trees to convert the slopes to fertile farmlands. Sheep flecked the grass, walking in single file along paths their small hoofs had cut into the sides of the hills.

'Motupipi goes from that point there,' Philip said casually, indicating a distant green peninsula on the right, 'to that wide bay to the south of us; you can see the boundary.'

She could indeed; the contrast between Motupipi's green acres and the straw-yellow of the neighbouring property's paddocks was blatant. Not enough fertiliser, of course. New Zealand was just emerging from a severe recession which had stretched the country's main export earners, the farmers, to their limits. Few people, Antonia thought a little spitefully, had the resources that Philip Angove could call on.

'Inland, our boundary runs along the crest of the divide,' he told her, pointing to it.

His hand accidentally touched her shoulder. Antonia froze; he continued speaking, but she couldn't hear the words above the beating of her heart. He seemed to fill the Land Rover, to loom over her far too close, far too big. She dragged in a shaky breath.

'So your land is on both sides of the highway, then?'

There was a moment when the tension seemed about to snap, until he said coolly, 'Yes. Angoves were here fifty years or so before the road went through. We'd get a better view if we climbed to the top of the hill.'

'Then let's go.' Anything to get out of the Land Rover and away from him.

It was a steep pinch to the summit of the hill, but Antonia was able to scramble up without the aid he offered her, even though a tingle ran through her body at the thought of accepting his hand. Playing with fire, she thought, torn between anticipation and dread.

At the top she stood with the wind moulding the material of her dress around her a little too closely for comfort, and looked her fill. Philip didn't seem to see any need to talk, for which she was grateful. Turning slowly, she drank in the view, using it, she realised with an obscure shame, to divert her attention from the man who stood only a few feet away.

No wonder he had that air of lordly command! Anyone who grew up in a place like this, able to lay claim to almost all the land he could see, would learn to believe that the world was at his feet.

He had carried the binoculars up from the Land Rover and was now scanning his acres. Antonia looked once at the arrogant, fleshless lines of his profile, then resolutely averted her face.

'All well,' he said, lowering them to hold out to her. 'Do you want to try them?'

'Yes, thank you.' They made an excellent mask. 'Do you always carry binoculars?'

'It's a habit my father had, one I've followed. You'll find that most people who live by the sea keep them handy.'

Antonia nodded. 'I suppose you get emergencies.'

'More than we should,' he said crisply. 'You need a licence to drive a car, yet any idiot can buy a boat of any size, get tanked up and take off without knowing a damned thing about his boat, the rules of navigation, or how bloody dangerous the sea can be!'

Antonia lowered the glasses. The expression on his face was forbidding, to say the least. 'There seems to be a change coming in the weather,' she said, wondering why she felt the desire to change the subject.

Faint lines crinkled the skin around his eyes as he scanned the thin, curly white streamers in the brilliant sky, and the thin, ominous wedge of much darker cloud on the horizon. 'Yes, a front's on the way. It's supposed to bring us rain. We could do with a couple of inches now and another two or three in a week's time to set us up for autumn. Seen enough?'

She nodded. Neither spoke as they made their way down the hill; he didn't offer his help again, although she knew he was watching her to see whether she needed it. It was chivalrous of him, but chivalry was an outdated notion, one that hadn't ever had much going for it anyway. It was essentially a patronising regard by strong men for weak women. Now that women had proved they could look after themselves it was no longer necessary.

Back at the house Mrs Angove joined them, flushed and a little heavy-eyed from a nap, on one of the wide, shady terraces that overlooked the harbour. A slatted roof was held up by more huge pillars, massive tree-trunks this time, smoothed but essentially entire. Brenda brought more tea, and after they had drunk it Philip excused himself and left them.

So Mrs Angove could continue charming? Stop being so suspicious, Antonia told herself. It was impossible to look at Moira Angove's face and suspect her of trying consciously to influence anyone.

'Paperwork,' the older woman said now on a sigh. 'John—my husband—used to hand everything over to accountants, but although they still do all the routine work Philip oversees it all. He was trained to run the business, of course.'

In spite of herself Antonia was interested. He was a complex character; he'd looked the consummate businessman in Auckland, the epitome of a man of the land on Motupipi... What hadn't changed was the iron-bound authority he exuded.

Idly she said, 'People tend to forget that all farmers have to be businessmen.'

'Of course they do, and Philip is very conscientious. That's his nature.' Another gentle sigh. 'He wanted to be an architect, but... Motupipi is such a big place, and of course there are the other businesses to look after, too, so a strong hand is needed at the helm. Philip understood, of course; like his father, he knows where his duty lies.'

Duty was a cold, if necessary concept. It made hard people, people with a certain ruthlessness to them.

'An architect?' Antonia couldn't hide the surprise in her tone.

'Yes. He'd have been extremely good.' There was an odd note in his mother's voice, almost of despair. Antonia shot her a quick, disturbed look, but the aristo-cratic profile was turned away, and when Mrs Angove continued it was in a light voice that was level and without stress. 'He designed this house to take the place of the old homestead, after it burned down.'

Antonia really was astonished. She found the house enormously impressive, perfectly attuned to the land and seascape, a restrained, monumental building that was at the same time a home.

'He's very clever,' she said, unable to repress the note of wonder in her voice.

'He's a genius.' Yes, there was that thread of emotion through the words again, close to pain. 'But he put his duty before his own personal aspirations.'

Much to his mother's dismay, Antonia concluded. It must have been a difficult decision to make. For the first time she felt a small sympathy for Philip Angove. Things had not always gone his way, it seemed. It sounded as though his father had been an old tyrant.

Unwillingly she recalled Mrs Collins's words. 'He hated the boy,' she'd said sadly. 'But of course he couldn't repudiate him. The Angoves don't cause scandals, not then, not now. Still, he got his revenge. He was a harsh man, John Angove. They paid, all of them, Kate with her life, Edward with exile and the loss of his son, Moira and Philip over and over again.'

Antonia's meeting with Philip's mother had convinced her that the whole affair had been a figment of Mrs Collins's imagination, but had John Angove believed it? It was an aspect she hadn't considered before.

A cold chill settled itself in the region of her stomach. She stole another look at Mrs Angove's serene, slightly drawn face. Had Elva Collins's obsession woken intolerable memories of past pain for her hostess?

Antonia was afflicted by a sudden pang of shame, almost as though she had betrayed Mrs Angove. It didn't help at all to tell herself that Philip had set this whole scenario up; he had deliberately manipulated her, hoping for this very conclusion, and she was behaving just as he wanted her to. All her righteous indignation, all her talk about ethics, couldn't prevent her from worrying about the effect of that wretched tape on the woman who was being so kind to her.

Mrs Angove chatted on, obviously enjoying herself. She managed to create the impression that of all the people in the world Antonia was the one person she would have chosen to be with her that afternoon, and that, thought Antonia, valiantly trying to view the situation with some of her usual cynicism, was no mean feat.

Because it was going to make her decision to keep the tape in circulation just that much more difficult to justify, even to herself.

I have to get out of here, she thought suddenly. It was all too much: the house, magnificent and serene overlooking its bay and the tiny, magical island, the broad reaches of the harbour, the frail and delightful woman charming her with that effortless ease—and the man who set her taut nerves jangling every time she thought of him.

Mrs Angove went on relentlessly revealing the sweetness of her nature, making Antonia feel less than the low, so that when Philip reappeared she greeted him with a desperate little smile pinned to her mouth. 'I'm afraid I'll have to go now,' she said, improvising freely. 'I didn't realise it was quite so late. I want to be back in Auckland before six o'clock.'

The green-gold eyes turned curiously opaque. 'Then you'll need to start almost immediately,' he said courteously, but there was something inflexible in his tone that made her bite her lip for a second.

It had become darker while she and Mrs Angove had talked, but, even so, she didn't expect the sky that took her breath away as she stepped outside a few minutes later. A solid screen of cloud had built up across half the sky, moving fast, the anvil-headed mass a shade of purplish black.

Philip said, 'You'd better stay until that's over.'

But she was determined. 'No, it'll be all right. It's not raining yet.'

'It's going to bucket down in a very short time.' There was a distinct edge to his voice. 'It will be dangerous driving through it. You might as well stay.'

Antonia shook her head firmly. 'I must go,' she said, hoping that the effort it took to smile at him wasn't obvious. 'Thank you very much, I've had a lovely day.'

His face was set into harsh lines. 'Don't be an idiot, you can't go out in that——'

'Of course I can!' The words flashed out, but died in a gasp as she was jerked to a halt by his hand on her shoulder.

'Shut up,' he said between his teeth, the words hard and jagged. 'Just shut up and get inside——'

Antonia never knew what possessed her then. She tried to wrench away, but when his grip tightened cruelly a wild impulse made her sink her teeth into his hand. The unexpectedness of the assault did the trick; the shock relaxed his fingers enough for her to twist free and race across the courtyard just as the first fat, cold drops began to hurtle down.

He shouted something, but the words were lost in the sudden drumming of the rain. Antonia wrenched open the door of her car, flung herself in and started the engine even before the door thunked shut. Thank heavens the motor caught the first time. As though the hordes of hell were after her she shot across the gravel and down the drive, shaking with reaction and shame, and the dreadful, sickening humiliation she had thought she'd left behind long ago.

He must think she was a madwoman! But she couldn't afford the luxury of regret and recriminations just yet; peering intently through the windscreen, she moaned softly at the sheer, brutal intensity of the rain, its savage fury. As she came up to the crossroads a bolt of lightning leaped across the sky.

She took a reluctant foot off the accelerator, noting with apprehension that the drains on the side of the road were already filled with tumbling water. Rain pelted down so heavily that none was sinking in; it sheeted off the paddocks in a great yellow flow.

Coming up to the corner, she realised that she was going too fast. Instinctively her foot found the brake, but although she barely touched it the car aquaplaned across the drive. Her breath hissed out as she dragged the wheel back. Nothing worked. The car kept floating and almost immediately she felt the sickening thump as the body side-swiped a low bank, forcing the bonnet around and into it.

Hurled against the steering-wheel, she was breathing in shallow, ragged gasps when the door was hauled open and Philip Angove loomed across her, rain running down a face dark as sin, soaking his hair to jet.

'Are you all right?' he demanded roughly.

Shock and pain made her light-headed, but she managed to nod. Nevertheless, his hands probed carefully, with skilled sureness. 'There doesn't appear to be any damage,' he said at last. 'Get out and into the Land Rover.'

Numbly, she obeyed. The rain was still hurtling down, dazing her with its ferocity. She had taken no more than two steps when she tripped.

Philip swore again, fluently but without expression, and caught her before she hit the ground, lifting her easily as though she were some small wild animal caught in a trap. And that was exactly how she felt. Chagrin and humiliation warred within, to be replaced by another, infinitely more dangerous emotion. For the first time since she had realised she had no one but herself to rely on, Antonia felt safe in a man's arms. It was as simple as that—and as weakening. Years ago she had learned the hard way that security came from within, not through a man.

'Have you hurt your ankle?' he asked savagely when he was once more in the Land Rover.

Staring straight ahead, she shook her head. 'No, I was just clumsy, I tripped. I'm all right.'

He directed a long, uncompromising glance at her. When her white skin was suffused with scarlet, he said grimly, 'Later on you can tell me what that was all about.'

Antonia clenched her teeth to stop them from rattling together. How could she explain? She didn't even know herself what had come over her. Her appalled eyes searched for the signs of her madness, and found them, a ragged half-circle of teethmarks on the fleshless back of his hand. Mentally groaning, she huddled into the seat.

Back at the homestead he manhandled her out of the vehicle and, scooping her up, ran to the refuge of a wide portico that led into the working part of the house, using the width of his shoulders to shelter her from the worst of the weather. Once inside the door he set her on her feet. Shivering, her pretty blue dress now limp and clinging to every opulent contour of her body, Antonia knew she must look a total fool.

She glanced up into an angular countenance slicked with rain, the sheen of moisture rendering the hawkish features even more dark and enigmatic.

'You need a shower,' he said impersonally, 'and a hot, sweet drink, in that order. Come on.'

'I'm sopping——'

'The floor will take it.'

Meekly, resistance dripping from her like the water, she went with him down a wide tiled hall.

Philip stopped at a door, opening it. 'The bathroom's through that door in the other wall,' he said.

Antonia walked stiffly past him into a large room, then stopped as her appalled gaze took in a huge double bed. Turning so sharply that she took him by surprise, she tried to struggle past him.

'Oh, for God's sake!' He sounded thoroughly disgusted. 'Get in there and shower. Believe me, if I had any designs on you I wouldn't be pushing them now. Brenda will bring you some clothes—her daughter's about your size—while I change in the cloakroom. Go on!'

'Thank you,' Antonia said, each word hurting.

'You need to get warm.' He waited but some inner conflict held her still. 'Hurry up,' he said evenly, 'or I'll come and shower you myself.' He smiled as he looked down into her horrified face. There was no softening in the crystalline beauty of his eyes.

'OK.' In spite of teeth that chattered and lips that were probably blue, she sent him a haughty glance before she walked across the several acres of floor, carefully avoiding the superb Turkish carpet that centred the room.

The bathroom was warm in spite of the marble tiles, with a huge shower big enough to take two people. Antonia's fingers had metamorphosed into fat, cold sausages which made it almost impossible to drag off her sodden clothes, and she was shivering so hard that she couldn't think properly, couldn't plan beyond getting some warmth into her frozen body.

Shock, she thought concisely. She couldn't really be so cold; she hadn't been exposed to the rain for long. As if to dispute this, another shudder racked her.

A knock on the door made her gasp and stare, but she relaxed when Brenda's voice said, 'I've got a few clothes for you; I think they'll fit, but if they don't I can find some others.'

'Th-thank you.' Still shivering, Antonia opened the door.

Brenda gave her an expert once-over. 'Yes, you shouldn't have any difficulty with these, but if you do, slide into Philip's dressing-gown. No bra, I'm afraid, Fiona's smaller in the bust, but she found a pair of bikini briefs she hasn't worn yet for you. I'll be back in ten minutes to make sure you're all right, and I'll pick up

your wet clothes to wash and dry them then, so they'll
be ready in an hour or so.'

Ignoring Antonia's stumbling thanks, she left. Antonia
waited until the door closed behind her before she
stepped into the warm water, groaning with relief as it
cascaded over her shaking form.

When she had finished dressing in the jeans and shirt
and jersey that Brenda had delivered, she stood looking
about her. The bathroom was incredibly tidy, but there
was enough evidence of Philip's presence for her to feel
an interloper.

Her reflection made her wince. The clothes were just
a little tight, and without a bra she looked overblown,
more than a little blowsy. Her hair had lost its pale
crispness and was now hanging limply around her face;
grimacing, she picked up a comb and tidied it. Without
cosmetics her white skin was an emphatic contrast to the
brilliant cat-slant of her eyes and the unusually dark
lashes and brows, the lush red contours of her mouth.
She looked untamed and strange, she thought despairingly after a last look in the mirror.

Halfway across the bedroom, she slowed down and
looked around. The room was huge, minimally fur-
nished with a bed bigger than any she had ever seen.
Covered in a thick eiderdown striped in blue and red and
beige, with big Continental pillows at the head, it was
made of some honey-coloured wood and shaped like a
sleigh.

Curtains of the same pattern as the eiderdown but
banded into checks framed a wide terrace overlooking
the garden and the harbour. Antonia's gaze was caught
by waves dashing themselves with insensate fury against
the rocks at both ends of the little island. Gusts of wind
howled across the water and smashed into the gardens,
ripping leaves and twigs free and heaping them in drifts
across the grass.

After a moment she turned away. She was almost at
the door when a roll of thunder broke sullenly across

the sky. The sound of the rain against the windows suddenly intensified as hail began to dance on to the ground outside.

Although the room was warm and all the chill had been showered out of her, a shiver tightened her skin as she stepped into the passage. Philip came towards her, lean and easy-gaited, his autocratic face set in lines of complete control.

He directed a long, unsmiling glance at her. 'You look better.'

'I'm fine.' But her voice had an odd little tremor in it.

He heard it, too. The level gaze sharpened until she thought she was impaled by crystals. 'Brenda's made some coffee,' he said after a moment. 'Come and have it. You're still in shock.'

'No, I'm fine. Just feeling stupid.'

There was no point in putting it off. She took a deep breath, but before she could say anything he interrupted in a voice that came perilously close to boredom, 'Hardly. A little dramatic, perhaps, but that seems to go with the gender.'

Antonia stiffened but he went on without missing a beat, 'I'm on my way to bring your car in. I don't know how damaged it is, but it might pay to consider spending the night here. If you have to get back I'll drive you down, of course.'

Without giving her time to reply, he pushed open the door beside her, ushering her into the room. 'Mother will be here shortly,' he said, and left.

There was no sound but the hail smashing against the window and her own ragged breathing. Antonia felt disorientated, a little sick. It was beyond her comprehension, this mindless, compulsive attraction.

Perhaps it was just the delayed onset of the well known spinster's itch, she thought savagely. It had to be confronted, and vanquished. Unexpected and strong the attraction might be, but she was not in the market for any sort of affair.

Because that was all it would be. If her brief, hideously disillusioning affair had taught her anything, it was that the Angoves of this world married women who came from the same background, not the daughters of farm labourers, however well educated and superficially sophisticated those daughters might be.

A small, bleak smile lingering on her mouth, she turned as the door opened and Mrs Angove came in. As if obeying some hidden signal, the hail eased into rain, and then stopped.

'My dear, what a nuisance,' the older woman said in her clear, warm voice. 'Never mind, you didn't get hurt, and we must trust to luck that the car's in good condition, too. Ah, here's the coffee; just what you need, I'm sure, after that nasty experience. When Philip comes back we can make a few decisions. Is there anyone we should ring?'

'No.'

Mrs Angove pressed sugar on to her. 'Lots for shock, you know; do let me put another spoonful in, otherwise Philip will be angry.' She gave Antonia a comical smile. 'And in this household we do our best not to make Philip angry. He has a fierce temper but he controls it so well that instead of boiling over he just freezes you through and through. He can be truly intimidating!'

The very thought of it made Antonia shudder inwardly, and certainly helped her swallow the sickly coffee while her hostess made her laugh and talk, drawing her out in a gentle, inexorable way. In her own fashion, Antonia concluded wryly, Mrs Angove was every bit as formidable as her son.

CHAPTER FOUR

BY THE time Philip came noiselessly back into the room the heavy cloud was beginning to shred and stray strands of sunlight were interspersed through the rain, teasing shimmering paths across the wide expanse of the harbour.

'Did you get my car? Is it all right?' Antonia asked carefully.

His wide shoulders moved in a slight shrug. 'You were lucky—it's not going to cost you much in panel-beating, but it needs to be checked over properly before you leave. The mechanic will have it ready for you by tomorrow morning.'

For a moment she didn't know what to do. Her indecision was plain to see, for his dark brows lifted and he said in a voice that held a slight taunt, 'You are, of course, welcome to stay the night. Or I could take you back to Auckland.'

Neither option beckoned.

'Of course she's going to stay the night,' Mrs Angove said placidly. 'It would be silly to go back—unless you have something to do tonight, Antonia?'

'No.' Furious at Philip's sideways, sardonic glance, and even more angry at her helpless flush, she finished lamely, 'Thank you very much.'

'No problem.' Although nothing showed in his face she sensed his unkind laughter. 'Come with me. I'll show you your bedroom.'

The bedroom was large with a view of a small, skilfully planted courtyard where bougainvillaeas rioted and a fountain splashed peacefully from a large glazed pot into a charming little pool. Decorated in cool blues and a subtle green, the room was serene and restful, as all good bedrooms should be. On one wall hung a painting done in naïve style of a view from an Auckland window with Rangitoto in the distance. Pert and charming, and very good, it saved the room from an excess of good taste.

It was as removed from Philip's room with its wild view of the harbour as anything could be.

'We eat at seven-thirty,' he said. 'Brenda will get your clothes to you as soon as they've been ironed.'

'Thank you,' she said woodenly. 'Or at least I suppose I should thank Brenda. There's no need for her to do them, though; I can.'

'It's part of her job,' he told her.

Her breath puffed out. Now, it had to be *now*. Tonelessly she said, 'I'm sorry I bit you. I don't know what came over me.'

Philip turned back. Her fantasies of him as a predator suddenly seemed all too close to reality, for there was a stillness, a waiting about him that sent her pulses sky-rocketing. 'Don't you?' His hard mouth curled into a knowledgeable smile. 'I find that hard to believe, Antonia.'

He wasn't going to make it easy for her. She said doggedly, 'Believe it or not, it's true.'

He lifted that brow, watching her too closely. 'You seem so composed,' he said thoughtfully, 'so completely in control, cool and aloof and detached. Then something ripped that carefully built mask away and for a moment I saw a woman as primitive as the thunder, as fierce and dangerous as the lightning. I plan to get to know that woman, Antonia, as well as the intriguing, sophisticated woman who lives behind that fascinating face with her.'

'No——'

But when he looked at her she could only shake her head. 'We'll talk about it when you're a little less shaken,' he said, and walked out before she could say any more, closing the door firmly behind him.

Totally unnerved, Antonia paced across to the window and stood for a time gazing out through the silver curtain of the rain at the flowers in the courtyard. Above the other wing of the house rose the sharp silhouette of a hill. Her pulse beating a rapid tattoo in her eardrums, she turned back to the lovely, peaceful room. The air in the room pressed heavily about her, stifling her, while a half-fearful, uncontrollable anticipation heated her bloodstream.

By seven the rain had completely stopped, leaving a sky of polished, tender blue. Antonia got into her newly washed and pressed clothes, wishing before she could stop herself that the dress was something sleek and sensual from a designer instead of pretty and practical from a good shop. It certainly suited her, lending a touch of clarity to eyes that were so dense with colour that they usually seemed opaque.

After combing her hair into place, she applied a touch of pink lipstick, a faint feathering of smoky violet eye-shadow, and she was ready. But she stood for a moment before the mirror, looking critically at her reflection in the glass. What did that instant leap of attraction mean? What caused it?

Some basic chemistry in the blood, perhaps, a cynical little joke played by nature. It wasn't Philip Angove's looks that tempted her so much as an inner, potent masculinity that beckoned in the most basic way to all that was feminine in her.

Had he been prey to such a sudden, all-consuming passion before? Somehow the thought of turning his life, his view of himself upside-down made her feel much more confident. If he, too, was wading through unknown waters, it didn't seem quite so bad.

As she came out of her room he walked around the corner at the end of the hall, dressed in clothes of such subdued elegance that they could only have been made for him by an excellent tailor. The white cotton shirt emphasised shoulders that were wide and muscular, while dark trousers revealed narrow hips and the long, heavily muscled legs of a horseman.

A sudden dryness in her mouth caught Antonia by surprise. Swallowing, she said, 'Good evening,' and could have died because her croaky voice gave it all away.

'Good evening.' His mouth eased into that smile that wasn't really a smile as he gave her a speculative look, green-gold eyes roving her face and hair.

She couldn't stop herself from searching out the dimple. It wasn't in evidence, but her eyes lingered on the crease in his cheek where it hid, and against her will she felt a treacherous softness assail her will-power.

He escorted her to another sitting-room that opened out on to a huge terrace, a room about the size of her flat, she realised a little hysterically, trying to conceal her preternatural awareness. 'What a lovely house,' she said chattily, despising herself. 'Your mother said you designed it.'

He looked angry for a moment, but almost instantly his features were wiped clean of emotion. 'Yes.'

Doggedly she went on. 'I was quite surprised when I saw it. It was silly, but I'd been expecting a Victorian homestead.'

'There used to be one here.'

Something in the deep, measured voice dragged her eyes back to his face. She said carefully, 'It burned down, your mother told me. It must have been awful.'

One black brow lifted. 'It was a blow, especially as we lost so many of our records.'

The historian in Antonia was horrified, but instead of being able to articulate her feelings more inanities came bubbling out. 'Oh, how dreadful!'

Philip said, 'The man responsible for it is now safely behind bars.'

Antonia was horrified all over again, as much by the flat savagery of his voice, controlled though it was, as by the arson. But she sensed that saying anything further would only make the situation worse.

Instead, she looked around the beautiful room, painted in a matt ivory that complemented the monumental style of architecture perfectly. White, she thought rather desperately, was not suitable for New Zealand's harsh, clear light; cream and ivory were ideal. Green palms and huge-leaved tropical plants and an antique Paisley shawl draped across one of the sofas added colour, as did a Persian rug, so old that the muted colours were a dim testament to splendour. On one wall there hung a painting, an abstract, powerful and haunting. Antonia found herself wondering whether Philip Angove had chosen the furnishings, or whether they were the brainchild of a good decorator. Had Tegan Jones done this too? If so, she had to be extremely intuitive, for the room's austere yet rich ambience was a perfect foil for the man who owned it.

'Can I get you a drink?' Philip asked, going across to a tray on which stood decanters. 'Wine?'

'Thank you.' And indeed for the first time ever in her life she felt she needed the temporary stimulation of alcohol.

He opened a chilled bottle of Gewürztraminer and poured a glass of the intensely perfumed wine, then another of sherry. Seated on an ivory leather sofa, Antonia waited, as edgy as though the next few minutes held the key to her future.

'I'm afraid my mother isn't joining us for dinner,' he said as he sat down. 'She asked me to give you her apologies.'

There was no condemnation in his tone, but Antonia sensed its presence. Anger and embarrassment mixed with chagrin to form a potent and totally unpleasant cocktail in her veins. She should have taken up his offer to drive her home!

'Perhaps I shouldn't have stayed,' she said, covering her emotions by taking a mouthful of wine. It burst into its characteristic fragrance in her mouth, evocative of the memory of past harvests. 'I hope I haven't made her tired.'

His wide shoulders lifted. 'Not at all,' he returned urbanely. 'She loves visitors; she's enjoyed entertaining all her life. Tell me about your job, Antonia.'

She obeyed, drowning out drumbeats of tension with the sound of her voice as she explained what she did. A good listener, he showed an intelligent interest in her work; she didn't have to explain much.

But all the time she expected him to say something about the tape. At last the tension screwed down too tightly; she said suddenly, 'When are you going to ask me for my decision?'

He leaned back in his chair, watching her with needle-sharp eyes. 'Testing me, Antonia? I'm not going to lie, I very much want you to erase that tape, but I told you I wouldn't harass you any further about it, and I'm not going to. However, I have the right to know your decision.'

'You know my decision,' she said.

He wasn't accustomed to being refused, but he restrained his swift anger. 'Very well, then,' he said calmly. 'How about editing it?'

Antonia caught back a sigh, understanding his request, wishing that she could give in and knowing that she couldn't. 'We don't edit. I told you that.'

His voice was even as he asked, 'Why?' He was watching Antonia intently, his eyes mesmeric, demanding. 'No one would need to know, no one but you. Would it be so hard to do?'

It was the voice of the tempter, the voice Antonia had heard him use to gentle the horse before he mounted it. He wielded it like a weapon, a subtle instrument of war, a seduction. It was difficult to keep in mind that he wasn't really interested in her, or only in the most basic, sexual way; he was using that instantaneous, blind attraction for his own ends.

She couldn't blame him for wanting to spare his mother pain, but some cynical part of her wondered how much of his concern for his mother's emotions was really concern for his own good name. After all, it must hurt a man of his pride to have the circumstances of his birth gossiped about.

She shook her head, keeping her eyes level and calm, letting him see that she was adamant. The silence crackled with tension. Then he said, still in that quiet, smooth tone, 'I can, if necessary, make it worth your while.'

Antonia swallowed. Desolation so intense that it was like the cold black depths of the polar sea gripped her. She couldn't drag her gaze away from his, but she managed to summon up enough resolution to let her contempt appear for a second. 'Don't try to bribe me.'

'It's no use appealing to your better instincts,' he said roughly. 'What else can I use but bribery? Threats?'

'Neither will make me hand those tapes over to you, nor edit them.' Her soft voice was even and steady. 'I can put a restriction on them, but that's all.'

Narrowed eyes never leaving her face, he shrugged. 'Ah, well, you win some, you lose some. It was worth a try,' he said indifferently, lifting his glass to his mouth. 'No hard feelings?'

It was an overwhelming relief to be released from the hypnotising snare of his gaze. Antonia said quietly, 'No hard feelings. I can't do it, Philip. It goes against everything I've been taught about being a historian. Elva Collins may have been repeating gossip, but it was current gossip. It may have some historical value. I can't wipe it just because it is untrue. It is part of her life; she said that she wanted to talk to us so that her daughter would be remembered.'

He closed his eyes, but not before she saw a bitter bleakness dull the glinting green. 'Would it be so dreadful if she were not?' he asked harshly. 'The long slide into oblivion has happened to most of the people who have ever lived. It will happen to her eventually, to you, to me. It's inevitable.'

'But that's one of the reasons why the oral history unit is collecting life stories, so that people's voices can reach out beyond the grave, so that they can live, be remembered, be people once more.' She leaned forward eagerly, trying to make him see what she was working for, the reason why she had to refuse him.

The beautiful mouth hardened. 'So that later generations can wallow in lies, malicious, evil gossip that stains the reputations of both the living and the dead?'

Antonia felt as though he had hit her. 'I'm sorry,' she said, reacting without thought to the corrosive scorn in the deep tones. 'Philip——'

'It doesn't matter.' Broad shoulders moved in a shrug. 'I told you I wouldn't harry you, and I won't. Let's leave it at that.'

Antonia sipped more wine, not tasting the fragrant golden deliciousness. 'I can understand how you feel,' she said, appalled to realise that she wanted to give in, to agree to his outrageous demand. Paradoxically, that knowledge stiffened her decision not to. 'Your family name is important to you, I know.'

He showed his teeth in a smile that sent a chill down her spine. 'Family name, family pride, family honour; they're considered to be outdated concepts now, but I was brought up to hold them important. And I love my mother. I don't want her to go through the whole vile gossip mill again. From things I've heard the first time was bad enough; it almost killed her, and in a way it spoiled my parents' marriage. My Uncle Edward thought the only way to deal with it was to leave New Zealand and never come back.'

'I'm sorry,' she repeated helplessly.

He looked his disbelief. 'Really?' he said in a voice tinged by a calm insolence that lifted her hackles. 'I suppose I should be grateful you don't think it's true.

Most people who refer to those tapes won't be so generous.'

'Do you really think that anyone will be interested?' she asked, anger making her less than discreet. 'I don't suppose many people in New Zealand even know who you are, much less care about thirty year old gossip. Every family has untold skeletons knocking about in their cupboards, and after a while no one gives a toss.'

'You don't believe that,' he said curtly.

'I do.'

For a long, chilling moment Philip held her gaze. In his expression Antonia could discern nothing but the proud arrogance she resented, and an icy reserve that shut her out.

Her stomach churned, and to soothe it she drank more wine. I'll have to stop, she thought somewhat fuzzily, setting the glass down too quickly. She wanted to convince him that she couldn't edit the tape and keep her integrity intact, but her thoughts were scattered, and she wasn't able to marshal them into any sort of order.

Anyway, another glance at the austere lines of his face made her uncomfortably aware that he had made up his mind. He would not understand her reverence for historical documents, which was what the tapes were.

Apparently he realised that whatever pressure he applied wasn't going to get her to yield, for he picked up the conversational beat without a pause, sliding into current affairs as though the tense little exchange hadn't taken place.

Caution spiralled through Antonia, but she relaxed a little. Clearly, he could be trusted—so far, anyway.

Once more he broke through her defences. In fact, so caught up was she that for minutes at a time she forgot that this man had tried to manipulate her emotions in an effort to persuade her into doing something she knew to be unethical.

A formidable man, difficult and complex. In some small way Antonia's outrage at the trick played on her by biology was appeased by learning that as well as the blatant physical attraction there were aspects to him she could respect.

'More wine?'

It was the last thing she needed. 'No, thank you.'

He got to his feet. 'Time for dinner,' he said. 'I don't know about you, but I'm hungry.'

The words, so simple and bland, set off little sparks through Antonia. In spite of a sophistication that seemed bone-deep, he had strong appetites. He also possessed the will-power to control them.

Brenda served a superb meal, after which they had coffee in the ivory sitting-room. Philip waited until she was relaxed before he asked, apropos of nothing, 'Is there a man in your life, Antonia?'

'A man?' Lulled by food and conversation and a second glass of wine, she looked at him blankly.

'A lover. A very good friend.'

He couldn't know how that hurt. Antonia replied with a cool, crisp intonation, 'No.'

'The consummate career woman.' Settling back against the pale leather, he looked down at the coffee-cup in his hand. Against the colourless walls his profile was a forceful silhouette, the beautifully sculpted mouth with its sensual lower lip slightly compressed in a smile that was pure mockery.

Something unchained, something feral and uncompromising, quickened deep inside Antonia. She wanted to lean over and wipe that cynical smile from his mouth in the most primitive way of all. She wanted, she thought with stark, disgusted honesty, to lie down with him on the sofa—or the floor—and make love until neither he nor she had the energy or the breath to talk.

Something of what she was thinking must have appeared in her face for he drew a sharp breath. 'Yes,' he said thickly.

Eyes fixed unwinkingly on his mouth, she watched as he put his coffee-cup on the table. Although common sense told her she should run, temptation whispered that just this once she would kiss him, and then she would know what it was like.

It was heaven. It was terrifying. Antonia had never wanted a man so much that every nerve was screaming for fulfilment. This was pure, stark lust, stripped of everything but the compulsive need to mate, to join with Philip so that nothing could come between them, to forget everything in the drive to sate the need that racked her unresisting body.

The muscles in his arms corded as they closed around her in a fiercely satisfying grip. His mouth was almost punishing, forcing hers open without hesitation, giving her no other option. Yet Antonia wanted that, needed it. Her response was every bit as ferocious, her mouth duelling with his in an age-old contest.

So far gone was she that when his hand moved to the long column of her neck she couldn't resist, smiling with a stinging scarlet mouth as his fingers slipped slowly down her throat to come to rest across the tumultuous pulse at the base. His glittering, heavy-lidded eyes were fixed on that thudding little traitor.

Antonia looked into a face drawn by unbearable hunger, dragging in a painful, impeded breath when she noted the colour flaring across his cheekbones, the sudden fullness of the mouth that had plundered hers.

With a shaking hand she reached out, her palm flat against the straight, taut line of his cheek. The olive skin was burning, hot as the flames that leapt like emerald fire in his eyes.

'God,' he muttered, cupping her breast, long fingers unerringly accurate as they homed in on the peaking, demanding nipple.

Sensation shuddered through Antonia, piercingly sweet as forbidden pleasures. She moaned, her body twisting with involuntary need, and went under, lost in the flood of desire.

He understood what she wanted from him, because he knew exactly how to touch her, with no cruelty, merely a dominating urge to make himself lord of her body. The bodice of the blue dress was stripped from her, pushed back so that the sleeves imprisoned her arms, holding her helpless beneath his gaze while he scanned her breasts, the heat of his survey raising the tiny prickles of scarlet across her milk-white skin.

She had never ached before, Antonia thought dazedly. Never. But she ached now, caught like a spark in the green-gold flames of his gaze. Hunger tore at her, pulsated through her, began in the fork of her body and relentlessly soared upwards.

'Why did you have to have a mouth like crushed red silk?' he said unevenly. 'Why couldn't you have been an ordinary woman, instead of desire personified, with your white skin and your passionate mouth and those eyes as dark and as turbulent as thunder clouds, wild as a maenad? Keats had it right, poor devil. La Belle Dame Sans Merci.'

He pulled her higher up into his arms, and at last his mouth enclosed the hard little nub of her breast that had been pleading for him for these last minutes. Stabbed by sensation, racked by it, Antonia cried out, torn to shreds by the ecstasy of his mouth against her unbearably sensitive flesh, tasting her, enclosing her.

He looked up, and slowly the blind hunger in his gaze intensified into a savage, mindless passion. At that moment he was man the hunter, the predator, intent on satisfying only the needs of his urgent body.

Antonia's heart stopped. Even as her body demanded the coiled strength and power of his she realised exactly what she was asking for.

Embarrassment crawled through her, driving the colour from her skin; averting her face, she pulled away.

She was afraid he might try to keep her imprisoned, but although his hunger was great his control was greater. He let her go, watching with a hooded gaze as she jerked free of him, her hands shaking so much that she couldn't drag the material of her bodice over her exposed breasts.

'Don't look like that,' he said in a level, almost toneless voice. 'There's no shame in what we did.'

Her breath caught in her throat. 'No,' she said numbly. Her fingers still refused to work; she fumbled uselessly with the buttons, until she said at last in a shaking voice, 'I'm going to my room,' and made for the door before she burst into tears or screamed, or both.

'Wait a minute,' he commanded, all traces of desire wiped from his voice, from his chiselled countenance as he got up from the sofa and came towards her.

Clutching her dress across her breasts, she flinched away.

He stopped as though she had hit him. 'Antonia, what is it?'

Colour rushed through the translucent layers of Antonia's skin, heating it to fire. 'I don't indulge in one-night stands,' she said tersely.

He just stood there, too close, not moving, but she could feel the activity in that cold, incisive brain. 'I wasn't planning a one-night stand.'

His voice was gentle, slow and smooth, and she realised in a moment of panic that he was speaking to her as he had to the horse he'd broken to his hand.

Wrapping her little remaining dignity about her, she backed away. 'I think we'd better stop this right now,' she said.

A sudden gleam in his eyes halted her. 'It seems to me to be effectually stopped,' he said, and smiled.

Oh, it would be so easy to give in to that smile, to let herself be persuaded by that damned dimple, but Antonia was far too strung up to trust herself to think clearly—or even to think at all. Forcing the words past her dry throat, she said huskily, 'Goodnight.'

And made her escape, walking with head held high and shoulders up so that he wouldn't see how humiliation had defeated her. She felt his eyes on her all the way.

Antonia didn't sleep much that night. The next morning she stared with dismay at the delicate blue shadows under her eyes. They were concealed with foundation by the time the housekeeper knocked on her door with a tray.

'Oh,' Antonia said remorsefully, 'I'm sorry, I meant to be out before——'

'No, it's all right. Philip has his at six-thirty before he goes out to work, and Mrs Angove never has breakfast, just tea and toast in bed, so this saves me setting the table.' She put the tray down on the table beside the bed, running her eyes professionally over the croissant and fresh fruit salad carefully arranged on delicate sprigged china. 'If you want anything else, tell me now and I'll bring it along.'

'I never have more than toast at home. It looks delicious.' Antonia smiled at her, relishing the aroma of coffee. 'Thank you.'

'My pleasure.'

She was nice, but Antonia felt as though last night's moments of madness were irrevocably burnt into her face, so that everyone who saw her would know immediately how wanton she had been.

How close she had come to compromising her principles, her whole conception of herself! Experience had taught her that sex was only worthwhile when it was accompanied by love; now, she thought with anguish, she had to relearn the lesson Bryan had taught her so well. If not restrained, passion could become such a driving force that it took over completely, subjugating principles, guidelines, self-respect—everything that made her the person she was—to the wild need to mate.

She had recognised Philip at first sight as a man who could make her forget the tenets she lived her life by. Common sense should have propelled her as far and as fast in the opposite direction as she could go. Only, of course, she had given in to that primitive need, telling herself that she was just experimenting when what she hungered for was the satisfaction of her needs.

At least this time she had been able to stop herself before she went too far. Now that she knew how dangerous Philip was she'd simply make sure she never saw him again after this weekend.

Wearily she got out of bed and went into the bathroom, where last night she had washed out her underclothes and hung them to dry on the towel rails. They were slightly damp; grimacing, she struggled into them.

She had just buttoned up the blue dress when there was a tap at her door. Antonia froze, but said, 'Come in.'

Her heart leapt as Philip came in through the door, dwarfing the room, draining it of light and colour by the force of his personality. He was in working gear, moleskin trousers that clung affectionately to his lithe form, and a black shirt with sleeves rolled up above the elbows, slightly sweat-stained. His raw, physical presence overwhelmed her.

'I'm sorry, I've been working,' he said calmly. 'I came straight in without changing because it occurred to me that you might try to run back to Auckland.'

'How can I? I don't even know where my car is.'

'It's in the garage. Leon Bolton, the mechanic, says it's fine—you've only put a slight dent in the mudguard. He's checked the whole thing over, and there's no damage done to the engine, although you're going to need new rings soon.'

'I know,' she said absently, trying not to look at him.

'Don't look so shattered.' The words were uttered in a calm, reassuring voice. 'I'm not going to throw you down on the bed and force you. But we have to talk.'

'There's nothing to talk about. I lost my head——'

He smiled ironically. 'Didn't you notice that I lost mine, too? As abnormal an occurrence for me as it clearly is for you.'

'Look, let's forget about it.'

His laughter was soft and a little cynical. 'Will you be able to? I'm damned if I will. Antonia, I know I frightened you last night, but you must have known that we respond very powerfully to each other, and did from that first moment we saw each other.'

She bit her lip. To admit to it was a step so irrevocable, so filled with apprehension, that she couldn't do it.

He lifted an eyebrow. Antonia glowered belligerently at him. And then he smiled. Antonia made a valiant attempt to cling to her anger, but it slipped away.

'It's better forgotten.' Refusing to look at him, she stared down at her small, pale bare feet.

She heard the shrug in his voice. 'I thought so too. But that's the coward's way out. I don't think I'm a coward. Are you?'

Don't use that voice on me! For a moment she thought she'd actually said the words. Bitterly, with Laurie Preece's beautiful face foremost in her mind, she muttered, 'I just don't want to get tangled up with you.'

'That was obvious right from the first time we met.' He sounded judicial, quite calm. 'What do you have against me?'

'Nothing!'

'So why did you take one look at me and decide you didn't want to know?'

'Look, I'm sorry if it wounds your ego, but I don't— I didn't want what happened last night, and I certainly don't want to—anything more like that.'

'You're afraid,' he said softly. 'Why, Antonia?'

'Go to hell!' Appalled, she stared at him, her eyes glistening like storm-drenched violets. A sob strove to break free; she took a deep breath and fought it back, calling on all her strength to give her some appearance of composure.

'No,' he said calmly, missing nothing, a smile quirking at the corners of his enigmatic mouth. He looked arrogant and calm and completely sure of himself, and she was suddenly afflicted by the old niggling inferiority. It made her go coldly, furiously angry.

'Damn it, I don't need this,' she suddenly shouted, horrified at her loss of control yet unable to do anything about it.

His smile broadened into a laugh. Driven mad by his composure when her world seemed to be collapsing around her, she turned on him with upraised hand and her mouth thinned into a snarl. His fingers caught her wrist in a numbing grip. He was still smiling as inexorably he pulled her into his arms, his narrowed eyes fixed on her paling face.

'You've already marked me once. Can't you direct all that aggression into more mutually satisfying activities?'

'I'm not aggressive,' she almost wailed.

The sardonic amusement faded to an inexorable, concentrated hunger that set something swift and fierce moving in Antonia's stomach. She tried to close her eyes, to blot him out, but the dark lines of his lean, angular face filled her vision. Almost hysterically she thought that she could smell him, that sun-warmed, salty scent of male, irresistible, potent as musk.

'Don't you dare——' she said in a harsh, tense little whisper.

'Don't dare what? Don't dare do this?' His mouth smoothed her temple in a lazy, light caress, yet the skin felt as though it had been burned. 'Why not, Antonia? It's just a kiss, after all.'

'You know why.'

His mouth moved to her eyelids. Heavy, waiting only for this, they fell. Tiny scarlet stars spun across her lids.

'Yes, I do know. That's why I'm here.' It was his wizard's voice, slow and deep and soothing, with a vein of sensuality like gold buried in a mountain's core. 'What's made you so afraid of this? It's the most natural thing in the world...'

His mouth brushed over hers, gentle, barely touching her sensitised lips, but after long seconds the tormenting, tantalising pressure eased. Antonia's lashes lifted, revealing brilliant slivers of colour. Heat ran in quicksilver fluidity through her veins, propelled by frustration, intensified by need. But he, too, was lost; the smooth, calculated assault on her senses was giving way to something infinitely less controlled.

'What the *hell* do you do to me?' he asked roughly, and then he kissed her properly, and once again she lost all grip on reality.

Almost immediately he tore his mouth from hers and stepped back, staring down at his hands, shaking slightly. Dazed and uncomprehending, Antonia touched her throbbing lips.

'God,' he said savagely on an indrawn breath. 'I didn't intend to do that. I wasn't going to touch you again until we'd had it out. However, I'm damned if I'll let you walk away from me. I don't know what the hell this is, but I'm going to find out. Can you ignore it?'

She shivered. 'No.' The word was barely audible. She swallowed and said more strongly, 'All the more reason to back away from it. It's just sex, that's all.'

'*Just* sex?' He was making a stab at his usual irony but for once it didn't come off. 'It isn't *just* anything! So you really are a coward, Antonia. Somehow I didn't think you were.'

Her chin lifted. 'I have a well developed sense of self-preservation,' she said shortly.

'You're terrified.' His eyes searched her face, stabbing, hard as quartz. Harshly, he demanded, 'Have you been abused? Is that what the matter is?'

'No!'

But the taint of the victim in her face, her voice, gave her away. He said softly. 'Who was it?'

Reacting more to the lethal tone, the sudden still threat that flowed through him like a hunter about to unleash death to his prey, than to his words, she said swiftly, 'It doesn't matter now; I had a bad experience, but he didn't beat me, if that's what's upsetting you.'

It didn't work. Still watching her with that absorbed, unblinking concentration, he said through lips that barely moved, 'There are other forms of abuse.'

He was learning too much about her. Desperately she tried to drag the conversation back into safer channels. 'I said it doesn't matter! And, yes, I'm frightened. I don't want an affair with you. I don't sleep with every man I'm attracted to—I have standards, and quick, easy affairs are not my style.'

'I'm not angling for a quick, easy affair. I'm not in the habit of sleeping with women I don't know and like and trust.'

'So you'll get to know me and then when you decide you like and trust me you'll sleep with me,' she said furiously. 'How kind!'

'No!' His voice cracked like a whip. For a moment he stared at her as though he hated her, his half-closed eyes as cold and hard as emeralds. Then he said on an exhaled breath, 'Let's start again, shall we? I want to take you out, do all the usual things that a man and a woman who are attracted to each other do while they find out whether the attraction is purely physical, or based on something more substantial. I have sufficient self-control not to leap on you, and, although I definitely want you, I don't intend to persuade you into my bed against your better judgement. Oddly enough, Antonia, I don't have to learn to like you, I already do.'

Which made her stupid heart leap like a just-hooked fish. There was nothing so seductive, nothing so calculated to appeal to her deeply hidden needs, as the simple assertion that he liked her. No other man had ever said it; it satisfied a lack in her that had never been appreciated before.

For a moment she hesitated.

The anguish of Bryan's betrayal and the loss of her baby had been so shattering that she had decided she would never love again, never be faced with the prospect of enduring that appalling pain again. So she had rebuilt her life carefully, and learned to enjoy her independence, her freedom from the risks of love and passion.

Renouncing her hard-won serenity for this dark magic would be completely reckless, stupid.

Because Philip wasn't talking marriage, or even any sort of commitment. He intended to move prudently, cautiously, towards an affair; that was obvious. He wasn't going to fool her, or trick her. No word of love would pass his lips.

She should be insulted. But erotic dreams had haunted her every night since the day they had met.

He fascinated her, entrapping her in a mysterious bewitchment. The proposition he was making would let her find out what her real emotions were. If she walked out of his life, she would always wonder what might have happened had she been a little more courageous.

For the first time she admitted that she wanted him more than she wanted peace, or freedom from pain; need ate into her composure like acid, destroying her pleasure in almost everything. Banishing him, even if he let her do it, would be the sensible, coward's way out. If she gave in to this passion she would learn where surrender took her.

Tiffany's voice sounded in her brain. Like Philip she had insinuated that Antonia was afraid, that she was turning her back on life, behaving like a coward. If only she dared to, she could embrace life and refuse to let fear rule her any longer.

Logic told her she was safe with Philip; she had already experienced his self-discipline. And her own, if it came to that. The night before she had been the one to pull back. But it was something other than logic that made her say, 'All right.' And the moment the words had left her mouth she was flooded by dismay.

His smile was ironic, yet understanding. 'Yes, it's quite a step,' he said. 'For both of us. Now, why don't you stay the rest of the day here? You don't have to get back to Auckland until this afternoon, do you?'

'No. No, I don't.' But she spoke slowly, for it seemed that she had handed over some of her autonomy to him.

'You can trust me,' he said.

'Yes, I know.' His perception chilled her a little. Instinct warned her to dissemble. She said with a glance at her dress, 'I'm heartily sick of wearing this. I really should go——'

He laughed. 'I'm sure Brenda's Fiona wouldn't mind in the least lending you shorts and a T-shirt.'

'Oh, no——'

But he said easily, 'And let's see if we can find a spare bathing-suit to fit you. We'll have elevenses first then swim before the sun gets too hot and burns that white skin.'

CHAPTER FIVE

A LITTLE while later, dressed in the height of teenage fashion for that summer—a baggy pair of scarlet shorts and a large red and white striped T-shirt—Antonia chose a bathing-suit from the number kept neatly folded in a large storeroom.

'Look, it's not a problem, don't worry about it,' Fiona Green said airily when Antonia thanked her again for the loan of her clothes. 'Mr Angove has been wonderful to us—there's nothing I wouldn't do for him. I'm just glad the clothes fit!'

It was clear that her emotions for Philip bordered on the worshipful. They seemed to live in some feudal time-warp here! The whole set-up was so far out of Antonia's experience that she was suffused by a sense of dislocation, of alienation.

After she'd chosen the bathing-suit and been given directions by Fiona, she went slowly along to the terrace and walked out into a day so fresh and idyllic that her spirits lifted, calmed. Suddenly her qualms and fears seemed small and petty.

The little island dividing the bay below was covered in trees, some quite tall. Cliffs laced with sprawling pohutukawa trees edged it, except in one place where a melon-slice of champagne-coloured sand faced the shore, curving in a way that indicated it was probably joined to the land by a sandbank. Nevertheless, the speck of land had the appeal of all islands, of loneliness, of romantic isolation where the rules of everyday life might be suspended.

It was very quiet except for the shrill zithering of the cicadas; Antonia couldn't even hear the waves hushing on to the beach.

Once again she was visited by the unnerving sensation of being dragged over an invisible boundary from her own world into another, where she was as innocent of the conventions as a child.

Her eyes roamed the gardens; some remnants of the Victorian plantings still remained, a huge Norfolk Island pine down on the shore, a sprawling flame tree close to a jacaranda, some ancient camellias grown into large trees. The grounds were already lovely, but once more she felt a gardener's itch to take them in hand and make them a fitting frame for Philip's house.

How could he have turned his back on his vocation? And what sort of man was his father to have demanded it of him? Certainly not a man who wanted his son's happiness, that was for sure. She was wondering what Philip had been like as a boy when her senses suddenly stirred.

'The island,' he said from behind her, 'is called Motupipi. The station took its name from it.'

Antonia sneaked a swift glance. He was looking out across the harbour, his features guarded as though he, too, was imposing a leash on his emotions.

She could think of nothing to say except for an inane query, but silence would have been too intimidating so she asked it just the same. 'And do you still get pipis there?'

'Buckets of them from the sandbar.' His gaze travelled down to her face, enigmatic, intent, the green fires smouldering but restrained. 'We'll go down and get some later this afternoon. You haven't lived until you've tasted Brenda's pipi fritters.'

'They sound delicious,' she said lightly. 'I imagine you must just about be web-footed, growing up here.'

'I certainly can't ever remember learning to swim. But I was sent off to boarding-school when I was seven.'

'Really?'

His smile was a little twisted. 'Don't look so shocked. I enjoyed it. For the first time I had playmates.'

'But surely there were other children on the station?'

He shrugged. 'My father had rather Victorian ideas on who his son mixed with, I'm afraid.'

In other words, as well as being the sort of domestic tyrant who expected his son to follow in his footsteps, John Angove had been an unregenerate old snob. Unable to think of anything that wouldn't sound as though she was criticising Philip's father, Antonia took further refuge in banalities. She asked a little diffidently, 'How is your mother this morning?'

His expression hardened. In a flat voice he said, 'Her usual cheerful self, although she's not going to get up today. She sends her apologies.'

Something already strained tightened another notch inside her. She said carefully, 'I hope she feels better soon.'

'She's just a little tired. She had a bad night.'

There was an awkward silence, one she broke by saying impetuously, 'I love this house.'

He sliced a razor-sharp glance at her, but when it was obvious that she meant it his mouth curled into a surprised but cynical smile. 'I'm glad you like it,' he said, 'some people think it too brutal, too stark.'

'Oh, no. It's magnificent.' Antonia gestured at the superb panorama before them. 'You had to create something that was monumental enough to cope with all this and not sink into insignificance, yet that harmonised with it. I think you've managed it perfectly. It seems a shame you haven't designed others.'

'I enjoy my work, and in spite of your flattering opinion of my expertise I doubt whether I'd have set the world on fire as an architect. My father thought it was a pleasant enough hobby, if a slightly strange one.'

Stifling a talent, especially one like his that amounted almost to genius, must have hurt him unbearably. The strong sense of duty that persuaded him to deny his vocation was a clue to the intrinsic toughness of his character.

'He sounds hard,' she said without stopping to think. 'And insensitive.'

'All Angoves are hard,' he said, smiling. 'It goes with the name, which means "smith". I suppose beating on an anvil for generations toughened us up.'

Antonia's heart lurched. There had been too much tension in their relationship until then for either of them to relax enough to smile like that, openly, freely, without reservation. For once Philip's elusive dimple was very much in evidence, although it didn't gentle the fleshless arrogance of his profile. Nothing, she thought dizzily, would ever do that, but it gave him a hint of rakish charm that made her suddenly see a much younger Philip Angove.

That smile sizzled right down to her toes. With something like horror Antonia realised she felt more for him than a casual lust which by its nature had to be transitory.

'Really?' she said weakly, trying to hide the shock of this discovery with banality.

'A smith was a man of vast prestige because he worked with fire and iron and strength to make things of great power. A smith had magic in his hands, and mystery in his knowledge. In Cornwall, which is where the name comes from, a county which was always poor in the material things, the smith in each community was a man of vital importance.'

'How far back can you trace your family?'

He shrugged. 'The Angove side? Four hundred years, that's all. If you're interested, I'll show you a copy of the family tree one day.'

'I'd like that.'

'There speaks the historian. My forebears wanted a new life away from the dead hand of tradition, but it wasn't as easy to struggle free as they'd hoped. Somehow they managed to reconstruct the bonds they had left behind them. Security has its disadvantages, one being the sacrifices expected of the individual members of a family.'

Warned by an austere note in his voice, Antonia said no more, but her understanding of him increased; duty was a poor substitute for a vocation. What other magnificent houses might he have created if he hadn't been the last Angove of Motupipi?

He went on, 'What do you know about your family?'

Was his heritage so important to him that he needed to match others against it? A glance at his face reassured her a little; he looked merely interested. 'My mother's family came from the Orkney Islands and settled in Southland. Mum was a nurse, working on the West Coast when she met my father. I have hordes of cousins all over the South Island.'

'All with the same Scandinavian colouring?' His gaze rested a moment on her fair hair, then moved deliberately to the high cheekbones, and from there to hold her eyes imprisoned.

She felt a fluttering in her chest, an unbearable excitement. 'No,' she said, trying to steady her voice, 'that came from my father's side.'

He got up and walked across to the edge of the terrace, long legs covering the ground in a stride that was all impatience. Antonia watched, her heart contracting with something like pain. It had been bad enough when all she felt for him was a resentful passion. Now it was becoming more than that she didn't know how to deal with it.

Such violent emotions were totally new to her. She hadn't loved Bryan, merely been dazzled by his sophistication and fooled by her hormones; the emotions he had roused were ignoble ones, conceit and pride and vanity, a childish need to be loved.

I am not accustomed to all this angst, she thought, mocking herself. For a moment she hated the snare of emotion she was caught in; it was degrading to be at the mercy of desire, all logic vanquished by need and hunger, those building-blocks of creation, primitive and irresistible.

Against the brilliance of the sky Philip looked like a hawk, the blazing green-gold of his eyes an astonishing, almost unnatural contrast with the dark, leanly honed features. He wasn't smiling, and the dimple had vanished. As though he felt her eyes on him he turned, and her gaze fell hastily to her hands, slim and tensely curled in her lap.

'Here's Brenda with the tea,' he said remotely. 'Can I ask you to pour?'

The fleeting rapport of a few minutes ago had vanished as though it had never existed.

'Are you sure you don't want me from now on?' Brenda asked, addressing Philip as she put the tray down. 'If you do——'

It hurt to see the genuine liking in his smile for the older woman. 'Of course we don't. You and the children enjoy the gymkhana.'

'Oh, we'll do that, don't worry. How's Mike?'

'Mike's had a relapse of tonsillitis,' Philip told Antonia. 'You probably noticed yesterday that he was nursing a sore throat. His wife said this morning that this time he'll stay in bed until she feels he's ready to get out.'

'These men who think the world can't stagger around unless they're there to give it a push! They just make things worse for themselves in the long run,' Brenda said forthrightly, adding, 'Are you sure you don't want me to stay with Mrs Angove?'

Philip shook his head. 'No, she says she's going to sleep all day so she can get up for dinner.'

'Well, I'll be back by six.' Brenda smiled impartially at them both. 'See you then.'

Antonia poured the tea, even ate one of the superb fruit and bran muffins; she watched with awe as Philip demolished three of them. Whatever work he had been doing that morning had used up a lot of energy.

'Where do you want to swim? Sea or pool?' he asked unexpectedly.

Surprised amusement glimmered in her eyes. 'You have a pool? With the sea at your doorstep?'

He grinned, but said amiably, 'My mother likes to swim, and it's good for her, but she gets cold quickly so I had a small heated one put in.'

Just like that. 'The sea,' she said, forced to face once more the difference between them. She earned a good salary, but a pool was beyond her financial reach.

After collecting a plastic bucket and the binoculars he seemed to regard as an extension of himself, as well as towels and a hat for her, they set off.

That untrustworthy rashness stayed with her, caused, she thought as she walked down the hill towards the little beach, by a combination of many things. 'Gather ye rosebuds while ye may, Old Time is still a-flying...'

How many women had read those pretty, seductive lines and gathered the honeyed flowers of passion, and how many had regretted it afterwards?

Probably, she decided, about the same number as had regretted not doing it.

'You have,' Philip remarked, 'an interesting line of hard-to-read expressions. What are you thinking of?'

'Rosebuds.'

He lifted his brows, something kindling in the depths of his eyes so that she knew he had taken the allusion, and cursed herself for being so arch.

'Indeed?' he said smoothly, an odd little smile pulling at the corners of his beautiful mouth. 'Their transitory loveliness, I suppose.'

Her eyelashes flickered. Hastily summoning her composure, she retorted lightly, 'Something like that. A warning to us all, that impermanence. Oh, look, there are birds working the bay. Is the fishing good in the Kaipara?'

It was clumsy, but he followed suit with the *savoir-faire* of a man whose courtesy was bred in the bone. 'Yes, excellent. I heard that a marlin was caught out in the Tasman several days ago, some miles off the bar.

Perhaps now that the drift-netting in the Pacific has been cut back we might see even more fish.'

Antonia wore the bathing-suit under Fiona's clothes, and he presumably had his on beneath his shorts. As they walked side by side through the lovely framework of the gardens she was visited by a full-scale, Technicolor image of how he would look naked, the purposeful swell of muscles, the flowing animal grace, the vital, powerful, controlled masculinity.

Explicit images set fire to her senses. She had to take a deep breath and rush into conversation. They talked of nothing much, but beneath the desultory words spun a thin thread of tension, keen and sharp, punctuating phrases, colouring their voices.

On the bank above the gleaming sand some Victorian Angove had built a delightful little pavilion, embowered in the blue and white puffballs of agapanthus flowers.

'There's a changing-room in there,' Philip told her.

Inside Antonia found a room containing three cubicles and a long mirror above a bench. It was as clean as the rest of the homestead, apart from a drift of fine sand over the tiled floor. She stripped off, hung her clothes on the hook in one of the cubicles, and surveyed herself dubiously in the mirror. The bathing suit was magenta Lycra; it was almost demure in cut except across her breasts, where it pulled just enough to make her self-conscious.

Shrugging, she went outside.

Philip was far too worldly to ogle; however, he certainly let her see that he appreciated the sight of her in it. Behind the smooth, almost humourless curve of his smile desire flared, stark and fierce, yet kept in close confinement by his will.

He was a formidable man, his appetites and emotions so rigidly restrained. What would he be like if something slipped the leash?

Better not think about it, she advised herself, blindly looking away from his lean, olive-skinned torso where hair curled in arabesques across his chest. The quick flick of her glance was a helpless tribute to his potent maleness in close-fitting swimming-trunks.

Compelled by the need to conceal herself before her body revealed in subtle ways—ways he would recognise, she knew—just how much he affected her, she ran down into the water, gasping at its impact on her heated skin.

Once submerged she revelled in its briskness. Philip clearly wasn't one for horseplay in the water. When he struck out for the island, Antonia went with him, enjoying the chance to swim without having to turn at the end of a pool. She was puffing slightly when they reached the other shore, but Philip showed no sign of weariness, although his chest lifted and fell rhythmically as he walked on to the warm, pristine sand of Motupipi's beach, sleek and gleaming as a god risen from the sea, water sculpting every sinuous contour of his body into a bronze statement of male perfection.

They walked side by side without speaking. Not a footmark marred the champagne sand except for the dainty inscriptions left by shore birds as they paced along.

'Oh, this is lovely.' Antonia sighed, looking around with dreamy pleasure.

He sent her a sideways glance. 'A woman with Tartar cheekbones and eyes shouldn't look so at home in the water.'

His gaze moved slowly and pleasurably down her body, lingering just too long on the soft mounds of her breasts. Little shivers chased themselves across her skin and she could feel the betraying tightening of her nipples.

'You promised,' she said sharply, turning away.

'I promised not to hurry you into bed,' he said. 'I didn't promise not to enjoy you. The way you look now is an invitation to sin in itself. I'm no eunuch, Antonia. You know damned well that I find you profoundly desirable, almost ruthlessly attractive in a way I've never experienced before. You felt it the first time we saw each other, just as I did, and you've done your best to repress it, just as I have, with exactly the same result. None.'

She bit her lip.

'I'm chasing you, Antonia,' he went on remorselessly. 'Run as fast and as far as you can, sooner or later I'm going to catch up with you.'

She flinched. His mouth compressed and for a moment that chilling remoteness was back again. Then he smiled, and his potent, reckless charisma washed over her like the seas of some faery land, at once hazardous and irresistible.

Antonia's breath locked in her throat. Swallowing, she tried to stiffen her resistance, and when that didn't work she ducked back behind the armour of unruffled poise she had worked so hard to achieve. 'I'm not ready,' she said honestly, her eyes smoky, her mouth held firm only by an effort of will.

'I know. I know it's too soon, I know it's too damned dangerous, but for once in my life I have to take the chance.' His tone was almost indifferent, but Antonia didn't make the mistake of underestimating him.

She said quietly, 'Just—don't rush me.'

Some undiscernible emotion glinted beneath his long lashes. 'No,' he said confidently.

Antonia's eyes followed the small droplets of water across his shoulders, moved to those caught in the fine scrolls of hair on his chest, lingered on the taut skin glistening over the ridged muscles of his abdomen. There was little to remind her of the sophisticated businessman she had first met. He looked like a man who wrested his living from an indifferent world by hard physical labour and the force of his will.

Desire glowed richly within her. For a frightening moment she thought she was losing her mind. His eyes were clear, sparkling green, the golden specks seeming to pierce her with hypnotic energy, enigmatic yet compelling, as though he was willing her to yield.

'I'm sorry,' she said unexpectedly. 'It's just that I'm nervous.'

'Are you? I wonder why.' His hands tangled in her hair, tilting her head back so that he could see her face, washed clean of make-up, naked beneath a searching, heated gaze that was lit by triumph. 'I meant what I promised. We'll take things slowly. All right?'

She nodded. Drying salt hardened into tiny crystals on her translucent skin, on the clear-cut red curves of her lips. Philip laughed softly, triumphantly, and kissed her, a mere snatch of a kiss, yet the dark tides pulsed up and through her body, and she swayed mindlessly towards him.

'No,' he said almost angrily and released her, stepping away. But he took her hand and like that, innocent as adolescents on their first date together, they walked up the unmarked beach with the dry sand hissing beneath their bare feet.

'Can we walk all the way around the island?' Antonia tried to speak normally, to conceal the bite of elemental hunger with a conversational tone.

'Yes, although not at full tide. It's too deep on the other side then. We don't have to worry about being caught now, the tide's just about on the turn. Do you want to go around it?'

'Yes. To satisfy the explorer in me,' she said.

The sand was packed hard and cool beneath their feet, inviting memories of Antonia's childhood when she'd walked the wild West Coast beaches and written on the sand with driftwood, long, unintelligible screeds before she was able to read. Her mother used to say she was a born writer; indeed, that had been her ambition until she was seduced by history in high school.

'Why the frown?' Philip asked.

Shrugging, she said, 'Oh, career woes.' By the terms of the trust the unit would close in three years' time, when she would have to start looking for a new job. She responded to his swift, speculative look with more than a hint of reluctance. 'Sometimes I wonder what I'm going to do when the unit disbands.'

'I see.' Stooping, he picked up a stone and skipped it out to sea, grinning a fraction sardonically as she applauded. When it finally plopped into the sea he asked, 'What do you want to do?'

'If this recession goes on it won't really be a question of what I want to do. I'll apply for anything that comes my way.' She was silent for a moment before finishing lightly, 'If the worst comes to the worst, I've kept myself by cleaning houses before, and I can do it again.'

She wasn't deliberately trying to shock, but it did occur to her that Philip Angove might never have desired a woman who made her living doing housework.

'Wouldn't you find such a life boring after a while?' he asked, his mouth quirking as though he understood and was amused by her desire to see how he reacted.

He was very astute. She laughed. 'Yes, I'm afraid I would. I do just enough housework at home to keep the place tidy and clean, but it's certainly not my favourite way of passing time. However, one thing about doing it for a living is that there's always a call for your services.'

'Well,' he said casually, 'I've no doubt you'll find something. Your c.v. is brilliant; I finished it with a strong desire to read your thesis.'

His nonchalant attitude reinforced the fact that he had nothing like permanence in view for them. Something close to despair clawed Antonia's heart, but she replied non-committally, 'Oh, I'm sure it would bore you to tears.'

'Why?'

She grinned. 'Because the status of women in the nineteenth-century peace movement is not exactly of wide popular appeal.'

'I,' he said serenely, 'am not the wide populace.'

He asked her a question about her thesis, and when she realised he was interested, not just pretending politely, she told him why she had chosen the subject and how interesting the research had been. Absorbed, they walked along the beach until they had gone right around the island. By then the tide was at its lowest, revealing the pipi beds that lay like some newly risen country, sleek and silvery in the sun.

Half an hour later, sandy and satisfied, with the plastic bucket full of delectable shellfish, they walked back to the mainland to the sound of the returning tide rippling past.

Antonia ran a finger along a faint tingle on her cheekbones and said regretfully, 'In spite of all the sunblock I slathered on I'm starting to burn.'

'Your skin is like a pearl,' he said, the words caressing her nerves. 'As soon as we get back on the beach you can put on the hat I brought for you. I should have made sure you wore it while we picked the pipis.'

'I'm quite capable of deciding for myself what I do.' His autocratic assumption that he could command her actions irritated her, but she spoke without any real heat. Sending an envious glance towards his olive skin, gleaming and naturally sunproof, she said, 'You're lucky, you don't need to cover up.'

'I do when I'm working on the station. And if you let yourself get sunburnt I'd say you definitely need a minder.' He took her hand. 'Come on, the tide is deceptive here—it seems to crawl in, but if we're not quick we'll find ourselves having to swim for it.'

'I suppose it's like that all over the harbour,' she said as they ran through the shallow water. Already she could feel the pull and surge of the current.

'Yes, it can be dangerous unless you know what you're doing.' He let her hand go as they reached the little folly of a bathing shed. Philip stooped to put the bucket down in the shade, but straightened abruptly, looking past her. He said sharply, 'Did you see that?'

'What?' Antonia followed his line of sight. Out above the water there glowed, brilliant even in daylight, the blatant crimson plume of a parachute flare. 'Someone's let off a distress signal,' she said idiotically.

Snatching up the binoculars, Philip swept the wide expanse of the harbour, his mouth a hard straight line. After a moment he swore beneath his breath as he lowered the binoculars.

'Grab your clothes and get up to the house.' It was a command, pure and simple, barked out in a tone that brooked no demur. Gone was the lazily indolent man of the past hour, the excellent companion. Swiftly Antonia obeyed; as soon as she reappeared he set off up the hill, his long, powerful legs moving so fast that Antonia had to run to keep up with him.

'What is it?' she asked breathlessly. 'What did you see?'

'People where they shouldn't be, along one of the sandbanks, the bloody fools. There's not a chance in hell of them getting back to shore before they're cut off. The incoming tide moves fast across those banks.'

'But they must have a boat,' she protested, puffing slightly as they raced up the slope. 'Otherwise they wouldn't have been able to set off a flare.'

'The flare didn't come from them. It was fired from the point that runs out towards the sandbank. An old chap lives there, a hermit I suppose you could call him. He hasn't got a telephone. Something must have happened to his boat, otherwise he'd be out there getting them in, but he did the next best thing and let off the flare. He knew someone would see it. People who live by the sea keep a good eye out for trouble.'

By the time they reached the homestead she was panting, but he seemed as cool as ever. He had to be made of iron.

Ignoring the sand on the tiled floor, he said curtly, 'You'll have to come with me. Everyone else is off at the rodeo except Mike, and he's in no fit state to help. Get into something a little warmer. I'll meet you here in five minutes.'

It took her precious seconds to drag her bathing-suit off and her underclothes on over her salt-roughened skin, but just as Philip carried in a pile of blankets Antonia arrived in Fiona's clothes, the hat jammed over her head and her sunglasses in her hand. He, too, had changed into shorts and an ice-blue cotton shirt with a navy jersey flung over his shoulders. They were the most casual of clothes yet they bore the same aura of elegance she had noticed on him every time she saw him. The power of money, she supposed.

'Right, let's go,' he said, checking her over with complete impersonality. She must have measured up for he nodded and led the way from the house, moving swiftly but with the loose, economical grace she would always associate with him.

Covered in dust, the Land Rover stood outside the gate. Philip drove it with controlled skill and far too much speed down the road to the other bay where she had seen him gentle the horse. Antonia gave a small squeak as he headed the vehicle straight on to the jetty, but subsided immediately, feeling foolish when it became obvious that the structure had been built to take it.

At the end he switched off the engine and leapt out, leaning into the back to pull out the blankets. 'Do you know anything about boats?' he asked as he set off towards the steps that led down to the platform where a scarlet, racy runabout was tied.

'Not a single thing,' she replied ruefully.

'Stay on the wharf. When I yell, let the lines off.' The platform turned out to be a pontoon, which rocked a little alarmingly under Antonia's feet as she followed him. 'Bow first, and then the stern. Jump on to the stern as you let that one off. Can you manage that?'

'I said I didn't know anything about boats,' she retorted with some asperity, 'not that I was a fool. Of course I can do it.'

His grin was sudden and amused, but brief. 'Blame it on your size,' he said, and swung into the boat.

Antonia removed herself to a spot by the bow. Hoping her fingers didn't turn into thumbs at the crucial moment, she flicked a glance towards the sea. Were they going to be in time? A nasty hollow feeling of foreboding in the pit of her stomach persuaded her to concentrate on the lines. The big engine muttered into life. Antonia bent and took up the loop of rope in her hands.

'Cast off at the bow!'

'Aye, aye, sir!' she muttered as she hauled the rope up. It was unexpectedly heavy, and she staggered a bit, but she managed to get it over the wooden post and drop it on to the deck.

'OK, cast off the stern.'

This was a little more difficult, but she wrestled it free and followed the rope into the boat, grabbing at the side as Philip gunned the engine and the runabout leapt forward, almost knocking her off balance. For a moment she clung tight, watching the wharf dwindle away behind them. Then she made her way towards the wheel.

Philip was talking into the radio, his profile carved in slashing lines against the brilliant blue bowl of the sky. Antonia noted the assurance in his hands, his face, realising that until then she had seen only part of the man. Into her mind there popped the recollection of him in the stockyards, a heroic figure from another age pitting his strength and his skill and his wits against the horse. He looked like that now, yet he was completely at home with the high-tech equipment of the boat. She swallowed to ease the sudden dryness in her throat.

In some ways it was simpler to deal with the sophisticated man of the world than the one whose raw power and competence jangled primal, barely acknowledged instincts, reinforcing that first, involuntary conviction that he was a menace to everything she had made of her life.

She could scoff, use logic to prove he was no threat to her, but her instincts knew better. Philip was dangerous because he challenged her knowledge of herself, and because he had the power to call forth a response unlike anything she had ever experienced before.

Antonia looked away to the bar, its turbulent water impeding the way to the open sea, hazardous even in these days of every modern safety aid. At least they didn't have to go over that, she thought with an inward shudder.

Although Philip threaded the boat between sandbanks with a skill that betokened complete confidence, many of the channels were still too shallow to take even the runabout's draught. At one stage they had to head directly away from the stranded group, but when they reached the end of the sandbar Philip swung the wheel and once more they were headed for the castaways. Antonia relaxed. It was clear that he knew the tangled, braided waterways as intimately as—as he would know his way around a woman's body.

Perilous thoughts, and to banish them she remarked on his knowledge.

'I grew up here,' he replied, squinting into the sun. 'I spent a considerable amount of my childhood either in the water or on it.'

From beneath the brim of the hat Antonia peered ahead. Even with her untutored eyes she could see that the currents were running faster and more vehemently. 'I can't see them,' she said, fear turning into stark apprehension.

'You're looking in the wrong direction. No, over there. Can you see them now?'

'No—oh, yes!' Such small dark blobs, barely discernible against the shifting radiance of the water, still so far away!

'There must be about eight of them,' he said, adding through his teeth, 'Bloody idiots.'

Antonia narrowed her eyes and peered again, but the tiny dark dots blurred and wavered in the brilliance, so that she was unable to separate out any individuals. He had to have the most incredible eyesight. Hunter's eyesight, she thought with a premonitory shiver.

'Why on earth would anyone stay out on a sandbank once the tide turned?' she asked, half of herself.

'God knows. The world is full of fools.' His voice was as controlled and as unforgiving as his expression.

A harsh judgement, but then he was a harsh man. A chill tightened her skin. 'How long will it take us to get there now?' she asked urgently.

'About twenty minutes. Long enough for them to drown.' His voice was level, utterly without expression, but she saw the white brackets about his mouth and knew that he was not as emotionless as he seemed to be.

'Have you had to do this before?' she enquired tentatively.

'Set out to rescue fools? More times than I care to remember.'

'Did any of them die?'

He flashed her a look. 'Yes.' The word was as hard and cold as a stone.

Without thought Antonia put a hand on his arm. She had been actuated by nothing more than an impulse of sympathy, but as his hand came over to cover hers and bring it on to the wheel a thrill of electricity ran from cool, salt-slicked skin up her fingers and into her heart.

'Let's hope it doesn't happen this time,' she said unevenly.

'They're still able to stand up,' he said. 'The water will be shallow over the bank for some time yet, but a strong rip will start to run past them fairly soon. Then they'll find it almost impossible to stay on their feet.'

Antonia shivered. As they got closer the tight little cluster on the highest point of the sandbar erupted into frantic waves.

'At least three children,' Philip said in a steady voice belied by the muscle flicking in his jaw. 'Not content with trying to drown themselves, they take their children with them.'

A cold finger of ice slid the length of Antonia's backbone. She would not care to have him speak of her in that tone. He was truly forbidding.

Throttling back the engine, he said, 'I'll go as close as I can to the sandbank, and they can come in over the side. I'll stay at the wheel to keep her in place, unless you feel you can do it?'

'I'd rather not unless it's absolutely necessary.' She felt in some obscure way as though she was letting him down, but it would be dangerous to say otherwise.

'All right. You'll have to make sure they get in quickly and with as little fuss as possible. Children first, and then the women. All right?'

'Yes.'

He gave her a look of approval that warmed her heart.

Antonia counted seven people in the water, four adults and three children. She hoped fervently that was the same number that had started out.

The note of the engine changed, subsided to a mutter as the boat sank back into the water. Carefully, skilfully, Philip eased the runabout up to the very edge of the bank, the muscles in his arms straining as he held the nose steady against the rushing, dangerous current.

Antonia was already braced against the side, holding out her arms for the children. But someone's nerve broke. There was a rush, and one of the men slipped and fell. A woman's high scream made Antonia jump. The current had the man in its grip, carrying him with horrifying speed down the channel. Someone yelled, 'He can't swim!' and the woman shrieked again.

Instantly Philip gunned the engine, surging past the small huddled group. Even through the sudden kick of horror in her stomach Antonia noticed that he was careful to keep the wake away from the group on the bank. The man's cries had stopped; he was, she realised with sick despair, being dragged under by the remorseless current.

'No,' she whispered, 'oh, no, please.' Her fingers fumbled with the fastenings of a life preserver. It seemed to take forever to get it free, but as Philip brought the boat up in front of the drowning man she threw it in, watching with wide eyes until she realised it was within his reach.

'Grab it,' she yelled, when he took no notice.

Antonia saw his face as he went down again, the features contorted into a dreadful grimace, desperation and terror making him seem almost inhuman as he flailed about. Instinctively she leaned out, but cruel fingers on her upper arm hauled her back.

'Hold the wheel,' Philip said in a voice that offered no alternative. 'Keep the bow pointed right there, at the point where the bar runs on to the end of South Head. Whatever you do, don't let the bloody thing go.'

CHAPTER SIX

BREATHING deeply, Antonia seized the wheel and tried to stop it bucking and kicking like a live thing. With hands that shook and sweaty palms she fought it into obedience. The hill that was South Head danced in her vision; she tossed her head back to get rid of a lock of hair over her eyes and concentrated more fiercely than she had ever before in her life.

Slowly she brought the bow around, wincing at the savage lash of a current that seemed to be pulling more strongly every second.

When she was confident she had it under control she spared a quick glance over her shoulder, just in time to see the panic-stricken man grasp Philip's arm and cling on with frantic hands and the hysterical strength of fear. Philip shouted something, and for an appalling moment Antonia thought he was going to be jerked over the side.

'Oh, God,' she whispered. 'No, oh, no, please...'

She wanted to look away, but her gaze was fastened painfully on to the scene behind her. The man in the water refused to let go; in a few seconds he'd drag Philip off balance. Teeth bared like a wild animal, no longer capable of responding to reason, he shifted his hold, but only to hook his arm around Philip's neck, pulling him even more precariously off balance. He clung with the merciless strength of a man who saw death before his eyes.

The muscles in Philip's arms knotted with strain; his hand moved with blurred speed in a short, chopping blow across the side of the drowning man's throat. Instantly that killer grip slackened; with a look of great surprise he began to slide back, but even as Antonia sucked in a horrified breath Philip flicked a loop of rope into the water just in front of him.

'Hang on,' Philip ordered, a whipcrack of sound, leaning precariously out to grab the collar of the other man's shirt.

The man in the water made no attempt to grab the rope. Philip yelled something else in his ear, and his arms and shoulders grew rigid with the effort he was expending. The drowning man's eyes opened; more by good luck than good management, it seemed, one of his hands brushed against the rope. Instinctively the fingers crooked, and, with the same death clutch he'd used on Philip, they fastened on to the loop.

Philip straightened up. Antonia saw a white flash of teeth in his tanned face as he began to pull the rope and its burden in.

Antonia was sure her own arms and back ached by the time Philip dragged the man over the side of the runabout. There was a final almighty heave when she expected to hear the corded muscles and sinews crack, then in a tumble of water and movement the rescued man arrived gasping and retching in the bottom of the craft. Immediately Philip leapt for the wheel and sent the runabout whirling; a second later they were surging back to the people on the sandbar.

Antonia drew a ragged breath of pain. He had pushed her out of the way so quickly that she had fallen against the side of the boat and some metal piece of equipment bruised her hip.

'Sorry,' he said through his teeth.

'It's all right.' Stepping over the sodden man in the bottom of the boat, she readied herself to help the others in.

A child in her arms, the woman who had screamed tried to rush towards them, and the inevitable happened; she, too, tripped. Antonia caught her before she went under, yanking both her and the child aboard with scant regard for bruises or pain.

The two older adults, in their fifties, Antonia guessed, handed over the other children, before carefully clambering in. Seemingly dazed, they sat without speaking on the seats along the cockpit, huddling the children to them while the younger woman crouched by the man rescued from the water as he struggled to his knees.

'Oh, Barry,' she wailed. 'Barry, try to get up——'

'Where do you want to go?'

Shocked by the hardness of Philip's tone, Antonia felt her hands slow as she wrapped one of the two little girls in a blanket.

The woman sobbed, 'McLeod's Bay. Do you know where it is?'

'Yes.' He turned the wheel, pointing the bow towards a small bay with a scattering of half a dozen baches along it.

'Barry, get up,' his wife urged.

Over his shoulder Philip said curtly, 'Stay where you are.'

The woman broke into noisy tears. Immediately one of the children followed suit. Feeling rather like an unsympathetic and unkind headmistress, Antonia said quickly as she draped a blanket around the man on the floor, 'You'll feel much better when you're safely ashore.'

'It's all right for you,' the woman wept. Another child began to wail.

Antonia retorted with crisp emphasis, 'Please don't cry.' She smiled down at the bewildered children. 'You look just like Maori chiefs with your feather cloaks.'

This stopped the two weepers; the little boy said enthusiastically, 'And this is our war canoe, fast as anything.'

The younger man was being hindered rather than helped by his wife, who was still half sobbing as she arranged the blanket around him. Perhaps mindful of Philip's terse command, he stayed where he was in the bottom of the boat, staring at his rescuer with a stunned expression.

In spite of the blankets around them the older couple didn't look well; the strain of their ordeal was obvious in their pale faces and the shudders neither could control. A quick glance over Antonia's shoulder revealed that the shore was coming up quickly, although Philip had to follow a winding channel towards the bay.

Like birds on a telephone wire the children sat side by side, all fear gone now, watching her with bright, enquiring eyes. They were still bluish around the mouth and each small body was racked by shivers, she noted, looking up again to estimate the distance to shore.

'We're nearly there,' she said, smiling at them.

They smiled shyly back.

She inched her way forward to stand beside Philip. He gave her a fleeting look. His profile was carved in stone, implacable, unreachable.

'How are they?' he asked curtly.

'The kids are fine. They're being Maori chiefs in their feather cloaks.'

His face relaxed a little. 'Clever Antonia,' he said softly.

Something light and airy, so evanescent that she didn't know what it was, bloomed within her. She smiled up at him, knowing that her face was probably revealing things it would be wiser to keep secret, but unable to control it.

Hurriedly she said, 'Half an hour can make a lot of difference to the tide.'

'It can indeed,' he said evenly.

Her eyes met his in perfect understanding. Another half-hour could have added several more deaths to the Kaipara's grisly score.

Without further speech Philip took the runabout into McLeod's Bay, and organised their disembarkation. Barry Whoever-he-was didn't follow his family up to their bach, but stood with antagonistic eyes fixed on the aristocratic blade of Philip's face. He had a sharp, truculent expression, the face of a man who habitually looked for insults.

'Yes?' Philip said coolly.

The younger man snapped belligerently, 'It took you bloody long enough to reach us. What the hell do you think you were doing, mucking round, back and forth, back and forth, when you knew we were in trouble? Bloody fishing, I suppose.'

There was an electric silence. Then, with such contempt in his voice that even Antonia felt flayed, Philip said softly, 'No. I was getting as fast as I could to a man stupid enough to go out on a sandbank with three small children at the turn of the tide.'

'We lost our bloody boat,' Barry shouted, thrusting his jaw forward, his face reddening under the hard scorn in Philip's eyes. 'The anchor came free and it took off before we even noticed it.'

'More stupidity.' Philip's tone was icy, each word distinct in spite of the fact that he hadn't raised his voice. 'The first rule of seamanship is that you make sure of your vessel. The Kaipara is huge and dangerous; treat it lightly and it will kill you. Your foolishness almost killed your wife and your children, as well as their grandparents. What sort of boat did you go out in?'

The younger man glowered at him. Clearly he was accustomed to people backing down when he attacked, but, more than aggressive enough to outface this man, Philip played by no rules but his own. He was forcing Barry to acknowledge how criminally careless he had been. Antonia felt sorry for him, for them all, but she understood Philip's reasoning. Better to suffer a dented ego than death.

'An aluminium dinghy with an outboard motor,' Barry answered reluctantly.

'How long ago did it slip its anchor?'

'About an hour, I suppose.'

'All right. I'll go and see if I can find it.'

'Easy enough for you to say,' the younger man snorted, casting a glance at Philip's runabout which he probably hoped was contemptuous but in which Antonia recognised envy. 'You've got everything that opens and shuts in that thing.'

Philip looked at him without a flicker of interest. 'That has nothing to do with it, and you know it. Next time you feel like risking the lives of your family consider that if I'd been in my office, which I might well have been, no one would have seen that flare, and you would all have drowned. They say that drowning is a pleasant enough death as deaths go, but I've seen enough drowned bodies not to trust folklore. It has never looked to me as though they died pleasantly.'

Shaken, but not wanting to lose face, Barry bored in again, taking refuge in banality. 'Who the hell do you think you——?'

Philip looked at him, and something in his expression cut off the pugnacious outburst as though it had been sliced with a knife. 'Go on up to your bach,' he said curtly, 'and while you're getting dry and warm try to think of a way to apologise to your family for damned near murdering them.'

For long seconds the younger man stood with gritted teeth, his eyes fixed on that proud, merciless face. By his sides his hands clenched tightly, shaking. Colour swamped his skin.

One lifted black brow was an eloquent commentary on Philip's thoughts. Humiliation complete, the other man turned swiftly and splashed through the shallow water, his back stiff with resentment and chagrin.

Antonia said indignantly, 'So much for gratitude.'

'That sort are bullies; they back down when they can't intimidate. Besides, he knows he was wrong. He'll never admit it, of course, but next time he might take a bit of care instead of assuming that anyone with the money to buy a boat is competent enough to handle it.'

Five minutes later Barry's wife came out with the blankets. 'Thanks—for everything,' she said diffidently.

'Just don't do it again.' Philip's voice was perfectly pleasant but Antonia wasn't surprised when the woman stepped back as though threatened.

'No,' she said. 'I'm sorry. We really are grateful.'

Philip started the engine, and as though the noise was a summons the children shot out of the small bach and waved enthusiastically. Antonia smiled, and waved in response, mildly surprised when Philip, too, waved.

'I was taught,' he said, looking sideways at her, 'never to be unkind to small children.'

She smiled, watching them dwindle away as the boat left the bay. 'Only to their parents. I hope they've learned their lesson.'

He shrugged. 'So do I, by God.'

'You were pretty tough on him.'

His shark's smile was hard and without humour. 'I don't want him doing it again. You did well. You didn't lose your head, even under fairly extreme provocation. I thought you said you didn't know anything about boats.'

'I don't.'

'Well, you knew enough to keep her steady and in place when I had to deal with our sullen friend.'

A dangerous sweetness flooded through her. Before she had time to give in to it she realised they weren't heading out to sea to search for the maverick dinghy. The bow of the boat was pointing towards the long spit of land just to the north of McLeod's Bay.

'Where are we going now?' she asked.

'To see why old Troy Hawkins didn't go out to get them himself.'

The hermit lived in a little hut barely visible from the sea, but he was waiting for them on the sand of the cove beneath it. He looked depressingly normal, almost dapper, for a hermit, Antonia decided as she scrambled over the side of Philip's boat. He was neatly shaven, and his trousers and shirt were clean and pressed. To be sure, the trousers were patched with a variety of colours, but the patches were skilfully set in.

'G'dday, young Angove,' he said, touching the brim of a non-existent hat as Philip introduced them. 'Miss. See you got them off OK.'

'Yes, no thanks to them. What stopped you?'

'Oh, blood-damned motor wouldn't go.' He sent Antonia a bothered glance, relaxing into a grin when he saw her slight smile. 'Just when you need the blood-blessed thing it goes kaput.'

'What's the problem?'

'Damned if I know.' He gave Philip a shrewd look. 'Damned if I know at all.'

Philip said calmly, 'I'll have a look.'

'Be glad if you would, mate, glad if you would.' He jerked his head towards his boat, hauled up on to the beach by an ancient tractor. 'Just heard on the radio that Sam Tucker picked up an aluminium dinghy with an outboard motor on it off Pohutukawa Bay,' he said as they walked across the sand. 'Probably belongs to that chap you picked up. Sam's got it in tow, and when he's finished fishing he'll take it into McLeod's to see if it's his.'

Philip nodded, but said to Antonia, 'You'd better sit in the shade. Your cheeks and nose are a little pink.'

So Antonia sat beneath a large pohutukawa tree while the two men immersed themselves in technicalities. For the first time she allowed herself to relive that terrifying moment when it had seemed that Barry was going to drag Philip into the water with him.

Of course she had been frightened. If he had succeeded they both could quite easily have drowned. Philip was an excellent swimmer, but even someone who regularly swam several miles a day would have problems with a terrified man in a fast rip. And if Philip had drowned the chances were they'd all have drowned, because none of them knew how to use the boat, or the vagaries of the harbour.

So her fear, she tried to convince herself, had been quite justified on a purely pragmatic level.

She was lying. It hadn't been merely pragmatic, that flash of utmost panic, those shattering seconds when she thought Philip could die.

And, although she had been worried about the other man, it wasn't the prospect of his death that had caused that moment of horror.

Before she had time to digest this alarming piece of information she heard the hermit ask interestedly, 'That your new girl? She's not as pretty as the last filly I saw you with, but she looks as though she's sweeter-tempered. Got to hand it to you, mate, you can pick them. Mind you,' he added reminiscently, 'I used to be able to pick them meself, once. Better make your mother happy and marry one of them one of these days, boy, or you'll end up like me, wishing you had a family to annoy the hell out of you in your old age.'

Despising herself for eavesdropping, Antonia strained her ears for Philip's reply, but he spoke too quietly for the words to be distinguishable, although she disliked the timbre of the old man's laugh in response.

'Well, don't be like me; don't go chasing the perfect woman. You'll never find her. There isn't one. And why should there be, when there's never been a perfect man? Anyway, you owe it to your family to get married and have a houseful of kids. Your blood's too thin—that's why you were an only child. Marry a peasant and get some good sturdy stock on her; that's the way to keep a family going.'

Philip's reply was short and succinct and again indecipherable, but it made the old man cackle delightedly, slapping his hand on his thigh while he let his amusement have its way.

Antonia didn't know whether to be furious with the hermit or approve of his practical outlook. Her eyes, deep and dark as amethysts in the moonlight, lingered helplessly on the absorbed face of the man who bent over the engine.

Philip was an odd mixture, completely at ease in so many worlds. Antonia's eyes assessed the way the sun caught in his hair, firing it with splinters of red, bright as the fire that melted minerals before they congealed into obsidian. His hawk-nosed profile was etched against the dark trees of the hill behind them, arrogant, authoritative. He was completely impressive, that air of reserve backed by a confident strength.

As she watched he found something in the depths of the engine. His expert, lean fingers worked for a moment or two, then held it up. 'There's your problem,' he said.

'Thought it might be,' the older man said instantly, 'but I couldn't get me fingers in there to see. I'm getting a bit rheumaticky, y'know.'

Philip grinned at him, and Antonia's heart contracted. Judging by the hermit's rather caustic remarks about the other 'filly', he had met Laurie Preece. Jealousy ate into Antonia, even as she told herself that Philip was too much male not to have had affairs.

Half an hour later Philip said, 'OK, that's it. Let's give it a whirl, shall we?'

'Fine, mate, fine.'

Philip straightened up, and came across to Antonia, still perched on her log. He was wiping oil from his fingers with what looked suspiciously like a handkerchief. 'We'll go out with him,' he said, as the hermit started up the ancient tractor. 'I think I've got it fixed, but I'd like to make sure, so we'll act as watchdog for a little while.'

'OK.' Antonia got to her feet, smiling a little ironically. If he had suggested in just such a casual way that they go to the ends of the earth, she had an ominous feeling that she would have given him exactly the same answer.

'Are you all right?' he asked, taking her by surprise.

'Yes,' she said simply, not willing to add anything in case she gave herself away.

He surveyed her face, his eyes sharp as a keen steel blade. 'Have you been bored?'

'Not in the least,' she assured him.

Her denial must have been convincing, for he said quietly, 'I couldn't leave him with no transport.'

'Of course you couldn't.' He possessed a sense of duty as rigid as his upbringing must have been. Or perhaps it was inborn, part of his heritage from those aristocratic ancestors who had begun as smiths, men of mystery and power and prestige.

Antonia's smile was mischievous. 'He's quite a character.'

'So you did hear him.' Something moved in his eyes. 'He sounds as though he has a stockman's attitude to marriage, but apparently he loved a woman he couldn't have, and because he wouldn't have any other he stayed single.'

Her eyes strayed to where the old man was manoeuvring his craft into the water. 'That's sad,' she said softly.

'Wasteful, too,' he agreed, his chiselled mouth slightly wolfish. 'He'd have been a good husband and father, in spite of the way her refers to women. He doesn't mean anything derogatory when he refers to fillies, or peasants.'

Antonia laughed. 'No? If we're going to use such old-fashioned terms of reference, I suppose you could call me a peasant.'

Amusement glimmered in his eyes. 'Of yeoman stock, surely,' he suggested gravely.

'My father was a farm labourer. "Peasant" is definitely the word.' She couldn't hide the flinty note in her voice. Bryan had made his opinions of her social standing offensively clear.

'Odd,' Philip said, his voice cool and considering. 'I'd have thought "thoroughbred" described you better.' He smiled a little crookedly. 'You have the fine bones and the elegant, nervous grace.'

'Built for speed, not for stamina?' she returned, rendered uneasy by something in his voice, in his eyes, something she couldn't decipher but which she sensed was not entirely complimentary.

'I'm going to have great pleasure finding that out,' he murmured, and bent to drop a swift kiss on her forehead. Her body tightened automatically, and as she watched him stride across the sandy grass she felt an ache deep inside her that she was beginning to recognise as frustration.

And with the ache came the fear, hard and heavy and darkly threatening, fear of losing herself, of becoming once more only a plaything as she had been for Bryan Howard.

But at least, she told herself as they whisked back across the harbour half an hour later, the throaty roar of the motor spilling out behind them, at least with Philip she knew where she was. There were no sweet, conniving lies between them.

It was something she clung to in the ensuing weeks as February ran down to March, and autumn officially arrived. The change of season made no difference to the weather, which was still sticky and hot, and no difference to Philip's attitude. They went out several times a week; he had, she discovered, an apartment in town where he stayed overnight as Tiffany and Eliot did. He never suggested they go to the apartment, and she wouldn't have gone if he had.

Usually they dined out, most often at small restaurants where the food was superb and the clientele discreet and select. And they talked. Antonia had never experienced it before, this almost obsessive desire to know about another person. She loved talking with him, loved the evenings when they were the last people in the restaurant, and still they talked while tired waiters joked in muffled tones behind the scenes.

There was no repetition of those searing kisses, for which she was grateful. However, he touched her all the time, a hand under the elbow, a quick clasp of her hand, occasionally an arm across her shoulders. Casual enough, yet each touch was imbued with an intimacy she found more exciting than when any other man had tried to arouse her. They kissed, too, at the end of each evening, but those kisses were light, almost friendly, just enough to send her to bed with frustration gnawing at her empty heart.

She no longer thought of Laurie Preece, until one day she opened the newspaper and there in the social pages was a photograph of Philip and the exquisite model draped elegantly over his arm, looking both smug and aloof. She was so beautiful that it was like a blow to the heart, her features arranged into a stunning, almost unearthly pattern of perfection.

Antonia forced herself to read the caption. They had been photographed the night before at a function opening a funds drive for a children's charity. Although she told herself that there was no need for all this drama, Antonia couldn't banish the jolt of betrayal that stormed through her.

It was not helped by Heather, who happened to look up just at that moment. 'Oh, have you seen the photo?' She got up and came across to lean over Antonia, gazing almost reverently down at the newspaper. 'Don't they make a fabulous couple?' she breathed.

Yes, they were perfectly matched, he so tall and lithely masculine, she reaching as high as his eyes and possessed of the physical presence to match his darkly dangerous magnetism. As well, they were matched in other ways. Laurie Preece came from a family as old as the Angoves; she moved in the same circles.

Agreeing took all of Antonia's composure. 'Wonderful,' she said, adding with a slightly lop-sided smile, 'Perhaps he should take up a job as a model too. He's intensely photogenic.'

'He couldn't do that.' Heather shook her head decisively. 'He's far too busy looking after all the Angove businesses.'

Antonia didn't bother to tell her she was being snide. Jealousy ate into her equanimity so that the future assumed the colours of a minor tragedy. Oh, stop it, she told herself. It was ridiculous to wallow in despair merely because a beautiful woman had her photograph taken with Philip.

Heather sighed and went back to her desk. 'She's outrageously gorgeous, isn't she? I'd give anything to look like that. I wonder if they are going to get married. Mum says that Mrs Angove would love them to—she and Mrs Preece went to school together and they're still best friends, you know? When you were up there did anyone say anything that gave you a clue at all?'

Heather assumed that the weekend spent at Motupipi was solely in connection with the unit, and Antonia hadn't told her about the subsequent evenings spent with Philip. It was too precious a secret. No doubt gossip would eventually filter back to Motupipi, but until then she was happy for no one to know about them.

'Not a thing,' Antonia said lightly.

'Well, no, I suppose they wouldn't let anything out; it's not as though you know them really, is it? And they don't go round talking about their business to everyone. They keep themselves to themselves, you know?' She wrinkled her nose. 'If anyone knows it'll be Brenda Green. But she won't tell anyone. She's a bit too up herself to talk to us peasants about what happens at the homestead.'

Antonia's brows lifted. She said drily, 'She'd probably lose her job if she did.'

'I suppose she might.' Heather considered this for a moment. 'Well, she would, of course! Philip expects complete loyalty from everyone. He's been very good to her, though. When her husband walked out on her... he was one of the shepherds, and a real hophead; he used to beat her up. Dad said Philip only kept him on because he was sorry for Brenda. Mind you, I think she was stupid! Catch any man using me for a punching bag! Well, when he took off, Philip wanted her to have him up for assault, but Brenda wouldn't. Anyway, Philip converted some rooms into a flat for her and her two kids at the back of the old homestead, and he designed a neat flat for her in the new house.'

And thereby gained himself an excellent cook and housekeeper in a country where home help was as scarce as hen's teeth.

Heather went on. 'She just thinks the world of him! Mind you, when Sean Green came back and set the place on fire Philip got the police on to him so fast you could barely see him for dust.' She shuddered pleasurably. 'I don't think I've ever seen anything so frightening. When the alarm went everyone went rushing across to get out as much of the furniture and stuff as we could. We got a lot out but Motupipi's so far from anywhere that by the time the fire brigade got there the house had burned down, because Sean had sabotaged the station equipment as well as setting fire to the house. Philip found him hiding in the hedge. I thought he was going to kill him. When Philip gets angry he goes all cold and controlled, as though he's iced up all through, you know? Honestly, it's terrifying.'

'It sounds it,' Antonia said mechanically, remembering the careless and unfortunate Barry.

'He looked at Sean as though he wanted to smash him into the ground. He didn't go red, he went completely white, and his eyes were all glittery. Sean had been quite stroppy until then, but once he saw Philip like that he shut up and started to look really scared. Philip just flayed him with his tongue until Sean took a swing at him, and then he knocked him down with one blow. I thought Sean would hurt him—he's huge, and he's known as a fighter—but Philip was so—so—well, graceful is the only word to describe him, and yet so *deadly*.'

Antonia didn't want to hear any more, but Heather was well away on her favourite subject. 'Philip had to give evidence, of course. Sean's lawyer couldn't get him off, even though he said that Philip and Brenda were having an affair, and that's why Sean lost his head. It was pretty awful, but of course the jury saw through that. Well, Brenda's OK, but she can't hold a candle to Laurie Preece.'

'Very few women can.' A kind of misery settled icily about Antonia's heart. It served her right for encouraging Heather to gossip. But the intensity of the feeling, and the grey smear of depression it left behind, made her aware of just how dangerous this delicate game was that she was playing with her emotions.

Sighing, Heather rolled her eyes. 'True, true,' she said, and went back to her work.

Antonia folded the paper with quick, decisive movements. She settled down to draft a letter, but after a second her thoughts slid back to the photograph. She gazed around the room; her eyes eventually came to rest on Heather's absorbed face as she indexed a tape.

On the Monday after the weekend at Motupipi Heather had admitted that she had been wrong to tell her parents; her loyalty should have been to the unit. It had clearly been a difficult decision, but by making it she had, with any luck, taken another step along the long line of difficult decisions that led eventually to maturity.

Thinking of Heather led inexorably to Philip. With an effort of will Antonia forced her mind back to her work.

He rang that night, and suggested they go out to dinner at what, he told her, was the best fish restaurant in the country.

'Aren't you too tired after last night?' Antonia asked dulcetly.

She could hear his smile in his voice. 'Jealous, Antonia?'

'Would you be jealous if you saw me in that same pose in a similar photograph?'

There was a short silence, as though she had surprised him. Then he said evenly, 'Your point is taken. Laurie and I were not at the reception together, and you're right when you call it a pose. She is a model. Point a camera at her and she automatically presents her best, most alluring side. I was just a prop. I'll pick you up at seven.'

She should, of course, tell him to go to hell, but she didn't. 'All right,' she said. If she hadn't been worried before at the violence of her emotions, she would have been then, for the relief that flooded through her was sweet and overpowering enough to set warning bells jangling.

She was being an utter fool going out with him. Why had she agreed? Because she was in thrall to the dark magic of his personality. She should know better—she did know better—but he was addictive. Although she still enjoyed the company of her friends, somehow she felt infinitely more alive when she was with him.

'Don't dress up,' he told her. 'It's a casual place, and we won't be late. I have to get home early.'

She chose jeans and a soft white cotton jersey which lit her skin to luminosity, applied the minimum of make-up and was ready when he arrived, tension still sawing through her. She believed him, of course she did; he had never lied to her. He had said that after she met his mother he wouldn't hassle her about the tape, and he hadn't. He had made no other promises, so she had no right to expect him to stay at home on the nights he didn't take her out.

Tiffany had told her he went out with other women. Was that what she was, a woman to take out on the nights he didn't go out with Laurie Preece?

She couldn't rid herself of a niggling uneasiness, based on nothing more, she told herself disgustedly, than Heather's gossip, and a photograph in a newspaper.

Tiffany had also told her that she still felt inferior, and in this instance her friend had been right; over the last weeks Antonia had reluctantly accepted the fact that Bryan's callous treatment of her had led to a deep-seated lack of confidence in herself as a person.

When she opened the door Philip smiled down at her and bent to kiss her ear, nipping the soft lobe with his white teeth. The unexpected little caress sent Antonia's nerves spinning.

'You look cool and sweet and fresh,' he said.

The compliment glowed through her, out of all proportion to its importance. As she went with him to the car she wondered with a shafting stab of anticipation whether it meant he was not going to keep that distance between them any more.

Their destination was a small, shabby beach settlement some miles past the outskirts of Auckland, and its old-fashioned, double-storeyed pub. In the surprisingly elegant dining-room they ordered crayfish and hapuku, with a bottle of New Zealand's excellent Chardonnay. Clearly the reputation of the establishment had travelled, for there were fashionably dressed people there, as well as ordinary families out for dinner, and groups from the bar next door eating a meal before they went out fishing.

About the only thing any of them had in common were the darting little looks the women sent, covertly or openly according to nature, across at Philip.

Antonia sipped some wine, not tasting the austere, oak-aged magnificence. Slowly, by some mysterious alchemy, her tension drained away, to be replaced by the keen, delighted anticipation she felt whenever she was with Philip.

'What do you think of the latest edict of the Arts Council?' she asked.

He lifted an eyebrow, but told her exactly what he thought of it.

She was well on the way to becoming dependent on his conversation, his presence. Well on the way? Why not admit it's happened? she asked herself silently as she caught him up on a point and queried it, her head tilted to one side, her eyes large and deep, veiled as the heart of a flower. A leaping warmth heated the pit of her stomach.

It was happiness of a rare and joyous kind to sit in the busy dining-room where the muted sound of the bar patrons drowned out the hush of the waves, and talk with that greedy absorption in each other she had never experienced with any one else.

When her meal arrived Antonia ate it with delicate enthusiasm, whole-heartedly endorsing the restaurant's reputation, even allowing herself to be persuaded into finishing with local Camembert cheese and biscuits and crisp, chilled green grapes.

Night had fallen when they walked out, but she didn't want to go home, and it seemed that he didn't either. 'Come for a walk along the beach,' he said.

As they strolled down the narrow, rutted road that ended at the wharf, he took her hand and held it in his big, warm one. Antonia let it lie there, unresisting. Mixed with the piercing need and the sensual awareness that kept her dreaming erotic dreams each night, there was this quiet, unfounded trust.

Of course it could be merely a matter of measurements. He was so much taller than she was, so much wider in the shoulders, so lean and strong and competent, and, although there were times when these qualities were a definite threat to her, at others like tonight she reverted to the primitive.

Big, brave, intelligent, responsible men, she thought with a flicker of self-mockery, had had survival value for the human species for untold generations. Naturally any woman, especially one who was small and physically unable to fight off the modern equivalent of a cave bear or sabre-toothed tiger, would feel more secure with someone like Philip beside her!

Because he looked as though he could cope effectively with anything that came his way. That male self-reliance and confidence was based on a dauntingly controlled violence, a predatory patience and alertness barely hidden by the civilised veneer. Philip might no longer be expected to protect his family from wild animals, but he was more than capable of dealing with one.

When she was with him she felt more alive, more charged with energy and vitality than she had ever felt before. She cast a swift little glance upwards, noted the arrogant, hawkish silhouette, and smiled. The words energy and vitality, however, reminded her of Mrs Angove, who had very little of either.

'How is your mother?' she asked.

For a second his fingers tightened on hers. 'She had a bad night last night, which is why I'm going home tonight. Apart from that she's fine. Her condition isn't life-threatening, or at least not immediately. It's cruel, nevertheless. She used to be very active. Now she's hard put to it to find the energy to get out of bed in the morning.'

'Those who have to just stand by and watch always find it wrenching.'

'You've been through something like this, I gather.' His voice was cool, almost distant.

'Not exactly,' she said with a small shiver. 'When my father left us my mother drank to dull the pain. She was doing a good job of killing herself when she ran the car into a power pole and finished it off quickly.' She felt odd telling him; she had never vouchsafed so much information about herself to anyone else. In a way it was a test.

'How old were you?'

'Sixteen.'

He stopped and turned her into his arms. There was nothing sexual about the embrace; he was offering nothing but comfort. Touched, Antonia leaned against him.

'You poor little scrap,' he said harshly. 'What happened to you?'

'I was lucky. I had a good friend, and I moved in with her family.' She was about to tell him that he knew Tiffany when he said quietly, 'Thank God for that.'

CHAPTER SEVEN

PHILIP released her and they walked on, still hand in hand, neither speaking. Contentment, pure and simple and rapturous, washed over Antonia. She could ask for nothing more. She had been truly afraid of the violent sexual magnetism between them, but at least she had experienced something like it before. This was new, unexpected, and shatteringly sweet.

Later, she realised that this was the moment she began to love him, as opposed to being in love with him. But for those exquisite moments she was idyllically satisfied to walk hand in hand with him through the serene darkness.

When the dew started to fall he said abruptly, 'We'd better get back to the car.'

On the way back he asked, 'When do your holidays start?'

'Next Monday.'

'Still going up north?'

She nodded. 'Yes. It's disgraceful, but I've never been further than Warkworth, and that's only forty miles from Auckland. I want to see the kauri forest, and find out whether the west coast beaches here are as magnificent as the ones where I grew up——'

'They have one thing in common,' he interpolated, 'they're just as dangerous. Don't go swimming unless you've got a local with you.'

She smiled. 'All right,' she said obediently.

'You're going to be away for a fortnight?'

'Yes. I'm spending seven days at a friend's bach, so I'll just laze about there. And if I don't get to see everything, well, it can wait until next time.'

'Sounds the perfect holiday.' But his voice was abstracted, as though he was thinking of something else.

Rebuffed, Antonia wanted to shout, Pay attention to me! Tell me you'll miss me as much as I'm going to miss you! But of course she didn't.

He said, 'I'd invite you home for a couple of nights, but it's not possible just now. We have family staying for the next few weeks.'

'I understand.' But that chilled her even more, underlining how very peripheral she was to his life when he was coming to assume a larger and larger place in hers.

Don't be an idiot, she told herself sternly.

'Where's this bach you're staying in?'

Startled, she looked up into his face. 'Oh, it's Tiffany and Eliot Buchanan's bach at Whangaroa. They own a farm up there on the harbour. A manager runs it, but they stay at the bach in summer.'

He looked surprised. 'I didn't know you knew the Buchanans.'

'Tiffany and I started school on the same day, and we've been best friends ever since.'

Frowning, he nodded. 'Does this farm have an address or a phone number? Just in case I need to get in touch with you?'

She gave him the postal address, wondering what would make him need to contact her.

Instead of seeing her to the door and then leaving, as he usually did, he came in this time, dwarfing her pretty little sitting-room. She made coffee and they talked desultorily while they drank it, until he set down his cup and slid his arm around her shoulders to pull her close, looking into her surprised face with glittering eyes.

Neither spoke, but excitement brought a soft pink flush to her throat and cheeks when he bent his head and kissed her.

She had been starving for this kiss, for this closeness, yet even as he expertly persuaded her mouth open she felt cheated, as though something was missing. Barely before her mind had formulated the thought she surrendered to the dark magic of his desire, lost in a sensuality she didn't understand, that had nothing to do with logic.

'Kiss me back,' he said thickly. 'Don't just respond to me...'

Antonia froze; she quite literally didn't know what he meant. Lashes that had fallen to veil dazed violet eyes flickered up. He was looking at her mouth with a raptor's intensity, something fierce and feral in his expression. She felt suddenly small and fragile against his hard, uncompromising masculinity, aware of his great strength and her own vulnerability, a vulnerability that was not just physical.

'Haven't you ever done that before?' he asked, the words slightly slurred. 'Are you a passive lover, Antonia? Show me what you want to do, what you want me to do.'

It was a fascinating idea, one that excited her. Reaching up, she traced the hard line of his mouth, feeling the clear-cut outline, the firmness of that full lower lip. With tingling fingers she sought out the crease that held his elusive dimple. He sat very still, watching her with half-closed eyes in which the glittering green and gold lights seemed to be concentrated into a colour so pure, so stark that it burned her.

Bubbles of excitement fizzed softly through her blood. She had never had the freedom to explore a man's body before. Bryan had always been the initiator, the aggressor; perhaps, beneath that swaggering confidence she had thought so sophisticated, he had been insecure, too young to have Philip's supreme confidence.

Or Philip's experience, a sinister little voice whispered in her head.

She ran her fingers down his throat, exulting in the contrast between the soft prickle of his stubble and the warm, oiled silk texture of his skin where his neck met his wide shoulders. Something moved in his eyes, and she remembered that for her that particular spot was especially sensitive; without thinking, her heart hammering, she lifted her face and bit delicately there.

His quick, indrawn breath told her that he too found it exciting. Anticipation warred with caution; the tug of desire through her body induced her to continue kissing the line of his collarbone to the place at the base of his throat where the rapid pulsing of his life force revealed that he was just as stimulated as she was.

But then she couldn't think of what to do next, until she slid her hand in between the buttons of his shirt and found the abrasive silk of the hair beneath, and the smooth, heated skin it sprang from, pulled tight over powerful muscles that were clenched into the involuntary stasis of expectation.

Her hand moved slowly, tentatively on, and came to rest over his heart. Absorbing its driving, savage rhythm into her palm, she spread her fingers wide, pressing them down against him.

A feeling of immense delight soared through her; she could do this to this clever, worldly man. And he trusted her enough to let her explore him like this, openly, without holding back. Only a consummately confident man would be sure enough of himself not to be hung up on a macho need to be the one in control. Ablaze with power, with fresh-born confidence, Antonia transcended her everyday self in this new and wonderful experience.

Slowly her heavy lashes rose; her gaze met eyes of such brilliance that they set her alight, and features carved darkly in angular lines of control. A small satisfied-cat smile touched the cupid's bow of her mouth, glimmered in the hot amethyst of her glance.

She undid several buttons so that she could pull his shirt back, and rested her cheek against his chest, glorying in his scent, salt and musk and masculinity. Her fingers brushing a small, hard nipple, she watched as the tiny caress lit a flame of need in his eyes, and, filled with daring, she bent and kissed it.

His breath lifted the wall of his chest. Again she glanced up, to see something like pain on his face. Alarm jerked her head away from him, but he caught her in an ungentle grip and pressed her back against him.

'Don't stop,' he said, his voice almost guttural. 'For God's sake, don't stop now.'

Her body was pierced by hunger, sharp, jagged shards of it cutting through her, pulling from the pit of her stomach, stabbing across her breasts, focusing on the juncture of her thighs.

'Philip,' she whispered, breathing him in, touching the sleek olive skin, tasting him. More than anything she needed to feel his hands on her skin, to melt into the strength of his body, enclose and enfold it and lose herself in him.

'Tell me what you want,' he said, control making his voice brutal. 'Tell me and I'll give it to you. Anything, Antonia, anything you want. You just have to ask.'

'I want you,' she said.

Something very like triumph touched the formidable line of his mouth, but it vanished so quickly that Antonia, dazed by her own audacity and the desire that gave birth to it, decided it couldn't have existed.

'And I want you,' he said softly, crushing her willing mouth beneath his. When she was still dazed from his kiss he flipped her cotton jersey over her head and expertly freed her from her bra.

Before her gasp had time to die he pulled her sideways across his lap, and settled her head against his upper arm. As she drowned in the scent and feel of him, he touched, lightly, tormentingly, the translucent skin of her breasts.

'There's a magnolia in the garden at Motupipi,' he said, his voice thick and distant, 'that has blooms the same colour and texture as your skin. It's the most exquisite thing. I've always wondered why I liked it so much, but it must have been because I knew that somewhere in the world there was a small Circe with eyes like crushed violets and a perfect, passionate, wilful little mouth, and hair like silken moonlight. Don't close your eyes, Antonia. I want to see you. Look at my hand, see how it looks against that white skin, those soft curves...'

He was pushing up the opulent weight of her breasts, cupping them, his lean hand astonishingly, barbarically dark against her flesh. Sensation ran riot through her, needles of heat penetrating with unbearable delight from her breasts to the secret, hidden parts that ached with an excitement intensified by a keen edge of frustration. Mesmerised by his touch, by the pleasure he was giving her, she squirmed against his hard thighs.

Shuddering, he bent his head and kissed her breasts, his mouth lingering against the skin. 'Don't turn your head away,' he said. 'Watch me, Antonia, watch us.'

Her mouth trembled; dazzled, her eyes glazed, she saw his mouth close on the budding nipple, and she cried out, a thin, aching sound that came without volition, startling her as much as the tempest of feeling his hungry mouth caused inside her.

'Yes, you like that,' he said quietly. 'What else do you like, Antonia? This?' His hand came to rest on the fastening of her jeans, pulling it down.

Body singing with need, with delight, she lay quiescent. She knew what was going to happen now, but she had neither the ability nor the will to stop it. Awed, even frightened by the ferocity of her response, she wanted him now, and here.

But accepting her need didn't stop the bitten-off gasp she gave as his fingers slid across her stomach until finally they touched the throbbing, heated heart of her sexuality.

'Yes,' he said harshly.

Shivering, she thrust her hips against the intrusive, probing fingers that offered so much ecstasy.

'You want me.'

'Yes. Philip——'

But he was withdrawing, covering her, his hands shaking but determined. 'No,' he said, kissing her disappointed mouth, her disappointed eyes, her aching breasts. 'No, I have to get back to Motupipi tonight, and our first time is not going to be a hurried, hasty coupling. You deserve better of me. I shouldn't have started this, but I'm tired of restraint, tired of showing you I can be trusted...'

She trembled with frustrated passion, her appetite for him whetted by the touch of his hand, his mouth. And suddenly the heated rightness of the moment fled, leaving her cold and ashamed and worried. As she struggled into the white jersey she kept her face averted, afraid of what she might see in his eyes.

'Don't try to hide from me,' he said firmly, turning her head with a hand along her jaw.

Colour washed through her fine skin and away again. She said stiffly, 'I'm sorry.'

'Why are you apologising? Because you were sweet and soft and willing and fiery? *I'm* sorry that I can't give you what we both want. I shouldn't have come in here tonight.' His mouth twisted as he looked down at her. 'But I couldn't stay away, and, in spite of the fact that I'm probably not going to be able to sleep tonight for frustration, I can't regret it. Do you?'

'No,' she said huskily.

He kissed her, pulling her against him so that she could feel the hard promise of his desire. When the kiss ended they were both breathing heavily.

'Torment,' he muttered. 'I'll see you some time this week.'

But he didn't. He rang on Thursday to say that his mother was not well, and that he thought it advisable to stay close to Motupipi. It was a peculiarly unsatisfactory call; there were noises of conversation in the background, and Philip seemed aloof, almost offhand. Antonia hung up with the old emotions of inferiority in full cry, unable to banish them even by recalling those minutes in his arms when he had encouraged her to make herself sensually free of his body.

Plenty of men had mistresses with whom they shared such intimate moments, yet their real lives were lived at home with wives and children and friends that the lover never saw. That had been exactly how Bryan saw her, not good enough for a wife, only suitable for using as a sexual plaything. His attitude had made her suppress her sexuality for years, determined never to allow a man to treat her with such degrading contempt again.

Now the old doubts surfaced. Was that what Philip wanted her for? Frowning, her mouth uncertain, she turned away from the telephone.

No; he was not like Bryan. She would stake her life on it.

It was something Antonia told herself each day of her holiday as she made her way up the coast. Pacing along the sweeping beaches, trying to walk off the nagging, bitter ache of frustration along miles and miles of sand where breakers roared in from across the wild Tasman and salt spume drifted like a thick fog inland, she repeated like a mantra that Philip was not like Bryan. He had integrity.

She tried to convince herself of it as she sat in the shade on startling white sand beside the Kai Iwi lakes, exquisite little blue-green gems in stabilised sandhills whose slopes were covered by grass and pines.

She repeated it as she drove carefully up the narrow, winding road that took her past kauri trees so immense and so old that it was difficult to look up at their flaked salmon grey trunks and massive branches and not think of prehistoric days when dinosaurs roamed the earth.

And she insisted on it when she came down the hill into the Hokianga Harbour, gasping at golden-ochre sandhills that backed a sheet of sparkling aquamarine.

Each day she missed him more; each evening she fought and subdued the desire to ring through to Motupipi so that she could hear his beloved voice.

And each night she dreamed. Morning after morning she woke aching and hot with frustration, snatches of images dancing in her brain, taunting her with their explicitness and their incompletion.

In spite of days that were warm and sunny and evenings hazy with a subtropical languor, Antonia's mind travelled far too often back to the night when she had forgotten the precepts she had chosen to live by and yielded to a firestorm of passion. It was only Philip's massive self-control that had kept her from surrendering completely, and they both knew it.

The holiday was all she had hoped for, a succession of days like jewels spent in surroundings of mostly untouched beauty. She should have been rested, thoroughly relaxed, but a nagging emptiness assailed her, and although she tried to ignore it she didn't seem to be able to banish it completely.

After meandering her way up to Cape Reinga, gazing with awe at the line in the water that denoted the conflict of the two seas, and with respect at the pohutukawa tree on the rocky, isolated headland from which departing Maori spirits were believed to make their way to the ancestral homeland of Hawaiki, she drove slowly down the eastern coast. A more gentle, feminine shore, it was marked by beaches shaded by the sprawling canopies of pohutukawa trees, and placid, enclosed harbours edged by thick olive-green mangroves, where herons dived into pellucid water.

Antonia delighted in this very different sort of beauty as much as she had in the wild west coast. Ahead were several days in the bach, set above a small bay of pinkish sand at the end of a long drive.

A mile or so before the turn-off to the farm she stopped at the tiny fishing and holiday port of Whangaroa to buy bread and provisions. As she piled the bags into the car she found herself hoping almost desperately that the days spent there would ease the savage restlessness that gripped her.

The bach was tucked against the side of a steep volcanic hill that reared up from the sea. Below the lawn convolvulus rioted down the hillside, its flowers as blue as heaven, until it reached the fringe of pohutukawa trees around the beach. The convolvulus was a weed, but, because Tiffany loved the flowers that turned to royal purple as the day wore on, the farm manager refrained from spraying the vines out, and merely kept them trimmed so they didn't invade the branches of the pohutukawas trees.

Antonia unpacked, discovered that the fridge contained milk and other necessities, put there on Tiffany's orders by the manager, and that the house was aired and clean. With a sigh of relief she took off the skirt and shirt she had been driving in, pulled on shorts and a brief sun-top and went to look out across the narrow harbour, gleaming like blue enamel in front of her.

She had been here once before with the Buchanans and adored it. Now, in spite of the heat and her knowledge that no more than four hundred metres away over the brow of the hill lived the farm manager and his wife and their three adolescent children, she felt cold and lonely.

Whangaroa Harbour, for all its beauty of high hills and landlocked waters, wasn't the huge sweep of the Kaipara, and, however kind the manager and his family, they weren't the one man she wanted to be with.

Irritated and impatient with herself, Antonia went down the path to the beach and stood in the shade of one of the trees. She would have a swim, wash the heat of the journey off her skin, then eat a very light dinner. Tomorrow, perhaps, she would climb St Paul, the volcanic plug behind Whangaroa township.

But her heart wasn't in it. She stood idly watching several gleaming big game fishing launches coming up the harbour, graceful, sleek, expensive craft, some flying pennants. Clearly the game fishing club at Whangaroa was having a tournament. As the launches disappeared behind the headland that hid the wharf of Whangaroa she turned away abruptly.

The sun had barely flamed down behind the hills in the centre of Northland when she went to bed. She woke in the cool grey dawn, listening to the silence as she despairingly tried to free her mind from the lingering, sensual aftermath of the dream that had plagued her sleep like an incubus.

After breakfast she went exploring. Her first find was a hammock in the garage. Working determinedly, she attached it to the hooks driven into the flame tree, and there she planned to laze the days away. But whenever she closed her eyes she saw Philip's face against the lids, drawn with passion, dark with demand.

A couple of days after she arrived the constant, nagging tension drove her to try the ascent of St Paul. It wasn't too difficult. In the final stretch she needed the help given by a chain, but she wasn't puffing badly when she got there.

Several other walkers, mostly young and speaking with German or American accents, had descended as she walked up and when she finally reached the top she was alone. Sitting down with a sigh of relief and a vow to exercise a little more consistently when she got back to Auckland, she rested her chin on her knees, letting the peace soak into her soul. From the pine trees in the plantation below cicadas sang a deafening chorus, almost blocking out the twittering of the tiny welcome swallows that swooped around her.

A monarch butterfly, brilliant in its orange and black livery, fluttered aimlessly by, reminding her that not very far away, according to the woman in the gift shop, was a bay where monarchs came to spend the winter, thousands of them drowsing the cold months away festooned over a huge pohutukawa tree in a tiny, north-facing bay.

It sounded magical. Antonia couldn't even summon up the desire to go and see the tree.

'Damn,' she said wearily. 'Damn the man!' and got to her feet, the magnificent panorama wiped of almost all its appeal.

In an effort to rid herself of Philip's ghost she went out that evening to dinner at the local pub, driving because the climb to the top of St Paul had left her tired and disinclined to walk the mile or so each way from the bach. It was early, so she was the only guest in the hotel dining-room, which suited her fine. But the lamb she ordered, although superbly cooked and delicious, couldn't tempt her waning appetite; she kept remembering the last time she had been in a pleasant, unpretentious dining-room like this, with Philip sitting opposite her, and the tempest of passion that had ended the evening.

A noise at the entrance to the room caught her listless attention. Colour drained in a sickening rush from her skin as her stomach dropped completely away. Headed purposefully towards her, striding with the even, determined gait of a hunter, was the man who had haunted her these past days and nights. Excitement and a searing anticipation brightened Antonia's face, turning her eyes huge and smoky, her mouth subtly inviting.

He had come for her, and surely, tonight, he didn't have to go home until the morning.

A waitress fluttered after him. When he reached the table he turned and smiled at her, and the woman went under without a gasp, helpless before the sudden, potent charisma. You and every other woman over the age of twelve, Antonia thought, but the momentary bleak cynicism was banished immediately by her singing, incandescent delight.

'Thank you,' he said, the crisp tone sounding completely normal. 'Could you bring me a menu, please?'

'Yes, sir.'

Swallowing to ease her dry throat, Antonia asked, 'Is everything all right?'

He looked tired, the gold leached from his eyes so that all that showed beneath those thick lashes were glinting green crystals. 'Yes.'

'Sir.' The waitress appeared, handed over the menu with solemn care, and recited the specials with her gaze fixed firmly on his face.

'The steak will do,' he said, cutting the girl short with pleasant finality. He flicked a glance across at Antonia's plate. 'And a bottle of Fumé Blanc. Cold soup for the entrée. Thank you.'

The waitress gave him a respectful smile and left. Philip leaned back in his chair and surveyed Antonia from half-closed eyes. 'What have you been doing to yourself?' he asked quietly. 'You've lost weight, and there are shadows under those amazing eyes.'

'I'm fine,' she said.

He reached out and took her hand, resting his thumb on the fragile blue vein that beat lightly, rapidly in her wrist. 'Have you been missing me?'

'How did you know I was here?' she countered.

He shrugged. 'I was on my way to the address you gave me when I saw your car here. Being extremely astute, I deduced you were somewhere around. So I came looking.'

The noise of a fishing boat chugging monotonously up the harbour broke into her thoughts. She glanced up at Philip's inflexible face then quickly away, her eyes following the boat, lingering on its wake as it spread out like a fan behind the craft. The flirting little breeze that

had cooled the day had died, and the water was a sheet
of jet with the great bowl of the sky darkening and in-
tensifying over it, stabbed by stars. To the north the hills
and cliffs stood out like the ramparts of some vast castle
built by beings large enough to ignore the tiny humans
scurrying around their feet.

'Why have you come?' she asked, not sure that she
wanted to hear the answer.

He said, 'We have to talk.'

'About what?'

The waitress fluttered across, set a basket of rolls in
front of him with a flourish and smiled. 'I forgot to ask
whether you wanted salad or vegetables with your steak?'

'Salad, thank you,' he said brusquely.

Four people entered the dining-room, bringing
laughter and noise with them.

'Surely there are more people here than normal?'
Philip asked.

'There's a game fishing tournament,' Antonia replied.

He looked across at her, his gaze moving from her
tilted eyes, dark between the thick lashes to the high
cheekbones that betrayed her with a hint of heat, and
the carefully disciplined curves of her mouth. He said
beneath his breath, 'I think we should concentrate on
our meal for the moment. We can talk about other things
later.'

It sounded more like a threat than a promise, and it
effectively removed the last remnants of Antonia's appetite. Philip demolished his soup with a healthy hunger,
discussing the ethics of game fishing now that most of
the fish were merely tagged and let go free.

Antonia responded somewhat randomly, still astonished at her reaction to his appearance. After the dish
had been removed from in front of him he leaned back
in his chair and scrutinised her, an enigmatic little smile
playing about the sculpted corners of his mouth. When
he had made her thoroughly uncomfortable he said,
'Now tell me about your holiday.'

Antonia matched his tantalising smile with one of her own, his provocation with her newly discovered feminine brand of the same thing, and noted with satisfaction the way his long lashes came down to hide his reactions.

A heady sense of power flared through her, heated and potent. Widening her smile a fraction, she told him what she'd been doing for the last ten days.

Philip refused pudding and coffee, and paid for both their meals. Made self-conscious by the impact they seemed to make on the other diners, Antonia was glad to get out of the restaurant, now almost full. It was, of course, the contrast between them, he tall and dark and dangerously patrician, she with her blonde hair and a face like a doll.

No doubt, she thought acidly, they assumed she was his mistress, or his secretary.

Outside a couple loomed up, said good evening and wandered past. A slight breeze rubbed the fronds of the phoenix palms together. Philip said impatiently, 'For heaven's sake get us to a place where we can talk without being interrupted or overheard!'

She said, 'I'll go first. We turn right just along here, then go on to the end of the road. A drive ducks off to the left. It's down there.'

Back at the bach they didn't speak, didn't even look at each other as they got out of their respective cars, but Antonia could feel his awareness like a flame beneath dark embers, only waiting for a chance breath to burst into searing life.

Half frightened, half elated, she went ahead of him along the narrow path. However, when they reached the door he said, 'I'll take the key.' His voice, aloof but quite determined, stopped any protest. Antonia handed it over and he opened the door and went in ahead of her.

Once inside he switched on the lights to look around the cool, airy house, moving with a precision that threatened her peace of mind. His well knit cohesion of muscle and bone was the foundation of his supple animal grace, and she was too acutely responsive to it, and to him.

'I'll put the kettle on,' she said swiftly, heading for the neat kitchen concealed behind the bar to one side of the living-room. 'I don't know about you, but I could do with a cup of coffee.'

She was babbling, and it didn't surprise her when he said abstractedly, 'Yes, all right.'

When she emerged again Philip was standing by the window looking down through the thickening dusk. She walked across and joined him. Lights began to twinkle across the narrow harbour, revealing the tiny settlements of Totara North and Saies, and the presence of isolated farmhouses among the hills.

Something slow and mournful moved elegiacally inside her.

'What are you thinking?' His voice was harsh.

Without looking at him she said, 'Oh, the swiftness of life, of youth—that sort of thing.'

'"Life's fleeting shadow",' he said, speaking with rough distinctness. 'Appropriate. Antonia, I came here for a particular reason.'

Antonia's heart stopped.

'That bloody tape——'

Antonia swung around. 'I should have known,' she said, heaven tearing to shreds on the floor, ripping all her happiness, her foolish, gossamer dreams. And then, reverting to the barely adult girl she had been nine years before, 'I don't want to hear about it.'

His hands fastened on to her shoulders. Grimly, speaking between his teeth, he said, 'You'll bloody well listen if I have to gag you! My mother is worrying herself into an early grave because of that tape. Your intransigence and insistence on your bloody professional ethics is making her life unbearable.'

'I told you——' she began numbly, so hurt that she couldn't think, couldn't find anything to say but a repetition of what she had already said.

His grip tightened cruelly. For a tense second he stared down at her, then flung her aside as though she dirtied his hands. 'I can get you sacked, and, believe me, I will, if you don't edit that tape. For God's sake, Antonia, I don't want you to erase it, just take out that piece of gossip!'

He was watching her with narrowed eyes, his face impassive, yet the menace was palpable, a cold and implacable warning that this man was not accustomed to being thwarted by anyone.

After a moment Antonia swallowed. 'I can't. I can put the restriction on it, that's all. Would it matter to her, twenty years——?'

'It does matter to her; she's desperate.' The gold-speckled eyes were the beautiful, soulless colour at the heart of an iceberg. In a voice that was all the more chilling for being calm and expressionless he continued, 'I can make it impossible for you to get another job in this field—or most others—in New Zealand, Antonia.'

'I don't believe this!' Once before she had encountered the wielding of power and money like a weapon to bludgeon her into submission. She couldn't give in, even though it was destroying her.

His smile was an icy parody. 'Of course I can.'

White-faced, numbed by an agony so intense that it hurt even to breathe, Antonia stared at him. It would be fatal to lose her temper; he was waiting for that, and then he would win, because he had no intention of losing his. But deep inside fury was growing, a smouldering primal emotion, fury with him for using her like this, and fury with herself for being so gullible. This time, she vowed, she would not be the only one to pay. This time he, too, would be left with scars.

'You have no right to threaten me.' Her voice was cool and distant.

He smiled cynically. 'I take the rights I want. But I never make threats I don't intend to carry out.'

Antonia saw herself reflected in his eyes, the cynical appraisal bruising her soul. All this time she had been falling in love, and he had been patiently, remorselessly hunting her down so that when he asked her again to edit the tape she would be so bemused by her emotions that she couldn't refuse. He must think she was nothing but a silly little blonde airhead. Once that was exactly what she had been, but she had grown up since then.

'I cannot and will not edit that tape,' she said calmly, and turned away.

'Oh, no, you don't.' He seized her arm. He had regained control of himself for his grip didn't hurt, but there was no way she could get free.

Antonia said nothing; his touch still sent electricity searing through her, but she was numb, she had to keep the anguish and the need and the rage under restraint. From beneath climbing brows she let herself look at the hand on her arm, then switched her gaze to his face.

'Let me go,' she said politely.

He showed his teeth. 'Do you find my touch so distasteful?'

Arrogant swine. And suddenly, in a malicious fire-flash of intuition, she knew how to punish him. 'No,' she said softly. 'I don't find your touch distasteful at all.' And she curved her hand around the stark line of his cheekbone, then slid it to the back of his neck and pulled his head down, forcing herself to smile, making the smile a promise of erotic delights. 'Not at all,' she breathed, wondering, too late, whether she had opened herself to the most crushing put-down of all.

She saw the exact moment his control cracked and the desperation surged through. Elation lit her eyes, moved her lips into a smile that was tauntingly provocative. Philip swore, then his mouth came down and crushed hers in a kiss that held passion and anger and betrayal.

There was no escape for either of them. She had known the first time she saw him that this was going to happen.

Later she would face the fact that everything else was all lies. Only this was honest, this raw, untrammelled hunger. His body could not lie, and neither could hers.

He kissed her with a need that should have terrified her, should have sent her screaming for help, but her response was as violent as his action, her mouth as demanding, her body as taut.

'I want you,' he said against her mouth when that first famished kiss was over. 'I've lain awake every night since I met you, wanting you. How can you do that to me?'

'I don't know.' On a broken breath she touched his cheek, found the harsh angularity of his jaw with wondering fingers. 'You've given me no peace, no rest, either.'

'I get drunk on the scent of you,' he said thickly, 'the feel of your skin, the drowning blueness of your eyes...'

He drew her hand over his mouth, his teeth grazing her skin with controlled savagery. Every cell in her body jumped, and the tide began to run, carrying her with it in a slow, honeyed sensuality. It wiped conscious thought from her brain so that she could concentrate on the clamour of desire that had been building these last weeks, building and building until now it roared away, an inferno, dangerous but irresistible.

'Yes,' he said, his eyes glittering green as wet grass in a thunderstorm.

He bit, not painfully, the fleshy mount at the base of her thumb. The roughness of his teeth and the unusual caress stimulated Antonia unbearably. She swayed, and he smiled and said, 'Why don't we sit down?'

Dazed, her brain drugged with sensuality, she let him pull her on to his lap on the wide, comfortable sofa.

'I love your skin,' he said against her throat. 'White as milk, smooth as warm silk. And eyes like a cat's, dark and deep enough to drown in, beckoning with a potent, slanting allure. You drive me *insane*.'

Delicious little chills chased themselves up Antonia's spine. Unable to stop herself, she sighed. Her heart was roaring in her ears, thudding fiercely in primitive need.

'Ah, yes, you like that, don't you?' Philip said. He tilted her chin and looked down into her face, his eyes narrow slits of emerald flecked by tiny gold flames, his jaw uncompromising. 'Do you like this, then?'

He feasted on her, slow, deep kisses along the length of her throat, tasting her with a gourmet's unhurried enjoyment, his mouth ravenous yet gentle, barely marking her skin. And as he kissed her his hand slid through the buttons of her shirt and found the soft mounds of her breasts, stroking in tormenting counter-point to the progress of his mouth.

Desire was a keen, piercing hunger Antonia could no longer restrain. She wanted him so much that her whole body suddenly arched, tightening into a bow of suppli-cation as she unconsciously tried to soothe the im-perative urge.

'Yes, you want me,' he said, triumph colouring the deep voice. 'Almost as much as I want you. Shall we do something about it?'

CHAPTER EIGHT

BESIDE the huge bed in the main bedroom Antonia stood quiescently as Philip's hands moved with deft precision, sliding her clothes from her. Lifting her high in his strong arms, he smiled as her head fell back submissively, revealing the lovely line of her throat.

'You're a creature of moonlight,' he said unsteadily, 'with your white skin and eyes the colour of a summer night, and pale hair like moonlight across the harbour.'

Then he set her down on the bed.

Unashamed passion darkened Antonia's slumbrous eyes as she watched him strip. He was magnificent, she thought dazedly. Like a statue, except that the olive skin was suffused with heat and the sleek, strong muscles moved and flexed in virile, potent life.

She held out her arms, running her hands with open admiration over his shoulders as he came to lie beside her. Beneath her questing fingers his pulse jumped; she found a pathway through the soft layer of hair on his chest, followed it down to the flat stomach, and the hard, heated promise of his masculinity.

'No,' he muttered.

She raised heavy lashes to look at him. 'I want to touch you,' she said in a smoky voice.

He showed his teeth. 'Touch me there and, God help me, I'll be no good to you for quite some time. Shut up and lie still—let me do this. Next time you can do what you want with me.'

Dazed eyes fixed on to the angular face, mesmerised by his dynamic male strength, she nodded, lying back against the pillows. Philip bent his head, capturing a pointed little nipple, suckling strongly until she cried out, her body arching once more in desperate entreaty. Heat

145

flamed through her in delicious agony, overriding everything else but the need that enslaved her.

Interpreting the small noise as a signal, he moved over
her and with one hard thrust of his lean, lithe body made
her his. For a moment they were still, frozen in a
breathless stasis. The simple, primitive act of joining was
enough until without volition her hips moved, enfolding
him, drawing him in. Groaning, he drove further into
her, as though he needed to bury himself so deeply within
that there were no boundaries, no way of determining
which was male and which female.

It was all magic, dark, primeval magic, the scent of
their lovemaking, her senses honed so that she felt his
weight, his forceful power, with a rapture unlike anything she had ever experienced. He knew exactly what
to do, how to touch her, using his formidable expertise
to wrench her from the world she had inhabited until
then into a new, ultimately perilous region where all that
mattered was the reality of two people moving together
in the compulsive embrace of passion.

Antonia's response was without limit, compelling her
towards some distant place, some destination so beyond
the ordinary that it was theirs alone. Two people locked
in the most elemental rite of all, they moved in age-old
harmony, mindless, wholly caught up in the moment.

Then Antonia reached that place, heard her voice
shatter as she crested some unknowable peak and was
flung into another dimension where ecstasy reigned, the
intense sensations shaking the very foundations of her
soul.

Before she had fully realised what was happening to
her he, too, sought that destination. He drove deep and
savagely and fast, his body glistening and taut, skin
slicked over rigid muscles, completely at the mercy of
his urgent drive for fulfilment.

She felt him against her and inside her, at her mercy,
slave to something he couldn't control, and the untamed
authority of his body was matched by the ruthless joy

that flooded her being, primal in its intensity, wholly basic. Suddenly he shuddered, his head flung back, and for long, timeless seconds she watched through weighted lashes as he was lost in his climax. At that moment, no matter what happened later, no matter that they both had lied, and her biggest lie was yet to come, he was hers.

Then he rolled over on to his side, dragging air once more into his lungs. Antonia shivered as the heat and the sweat of their encounter dried and faded. Her heart-rate sank back into its normal pace and the sensual exaltation ebbed to numbness. The enormity of what she had done flooded over her; with it, vast and encompassing, came anger and pain.

Disillusion was acrid in her throat, corrosive and inexorable. The rapture he had tacitly promised, the keen enjoyment in his company, the conversation and the sexual tension, all were bait for a trap set just for her. As soon as Philip had realised that intimidation and the power of the Angove name weren't going to get him his own way he must have deliberately sought her out, intent on seducing the wretched tape from her. He had had help, of course. Hers, and a cruel and capricious Nature, whose only aim was to produce children, no matter what it cost their parents.

Her blood ran cold. They had used no protection, none at all!

Oh, God, what if she was pregnant? What would she do?

Time enough, her rational self replied, to worry about that if it happened. For the moment she had to get herself out of this humiliating situation with as much dignity as possible. And that meant Philip had to get off this bed and into his clothes and out of the bach and out of her life forever. If he stayed much longer she was going to crack. That maddened union had cut her loose from the ground; made her stupid and trembly and afraid. And she would die if she cried in front of him.

With all her heart she willed him to get out of there. But he turned and pulled her around, tilting back her chin to expose her face to his gaze.

'What the hell is going through that brain of yours now?' he asked silkily.

She lifted her brows. She even smiled. 'I was just thinking that for a bastard you're a damned good lover. But that's it, Philip, once is enough. You can go now.'

His eyes narrowed. Green splinters stabbed her, probing beneath the precarious mask of her composure. 'What's this all about?' he demanded even more quietly.

She shrugged, faked a yawn. 'You wanted something from me, I wanted something from you. I'm afraid I can't give you what you want, but you've more than fulfilled any expectations I had of your prowess in bed.' Anger and bitterness prowled behind her words but not for an instant did she unleash them. Pride forced her to continue. 'You're a good lover, as I'm sure plenty of women know, but I'm not in the market for a long-term affair.' She even managed to smile, to lie with the flat ring of truth. 'I've just been offered a job in Christchurch, so it would have come to an end anyway. I'm sorry I can't censor that tape for you, but don't give up; you might have better luck with my replacement.'

He stared at her as though she had gone mad. Then his face darkened, the skin tightening over the arrogant bones, and something ugly moved in the depths of his eyes. Fascinated, terrified, she watched as his hands clenched at his thighs, then unclenched, clenched again. They were long and lean and they made very serviceable fists, strong, dangerous, murderous.

Heather's voice telling her of that sign of fury echoed in her mind. He had hit Brenda's husband...

Antonia shrank back, but he didn't touch her although he seemed to be looming over her.

'You little bitch,' he said softly, his eyes never leaving her face.

She laughed a little, striving for a note of irony. Fear tingled through her nerve-ends. But she was committed, she had to go on. Her determination not to let him realise how severely he had wounded her propelled the words from her mouth in a calm, almost amused tone. 'I enjoy your company very much, but I like my independence. Once bitten, twice shy, you know.'

Now why the hell had she said that? His quick, cool brain would immediately seize on such a revelation and use it against her.

But he ignored it. 'You're very good.' He sounded thoughtful, even judicious, as though he hadn't, only a few minutes before, been locked in the most profound embrace of all with her. 'So good that I want much more of you than the taste I've had so far.'

'No!'

Panic-stricken, she closed her eyes, and he laughed, a soft, cynical sound without an atom of humour. 'Open your mouth for me,' he said, pulling her into him.

She fought, but he was ruthless, and soon, without further resistance, her whole heart and body united in need, she followed where he led.

She woke to a tangle of bedclothes and an empty bed. The sun was high in the sky, and when she stretched she winced at the myriad small aches and pains that told her how thoroughly and well she had been taken the night before.

After a cup of ferocious coffee she went for another walk up St Paul, going far too fast so that she'd exhaust herself. Back at the bach, she collapsed into the hammock, closed her eyes against the dazzle of the glittering, dancing harbour below, and tried to work out what had happened, what it was that had tipped her so far off balance, just what the traitor in her psyche was.

What was this lust that made them, both rational adults, look at each other and desire beyond all rationality, want until it came perilously close to madness?

It was more than the fact that he was attractive to the eye. Other men were as handsome as Philip Angove, yet her pulse-rate had not increased a bit at the sight of any of them. Something in him, more elemental and more subtle than mere good looks, called to her with a siren's irresistible lure.

Whatever it was, she wasn't the only woman affected by it. His hard-edged, uncompromising sensuality, allied with the concentrated authority that crackled from him, made him a man women couldn't help but want. And the way he moved, Antonia thought dreamily. Silently, with the dangerous grace and leashed feline strength of a panther...

She shivered, arousal cramping deep within her. Who was it who'd said that Charles II only had to look at Barbara Castlemaine across the room to want her, in spite of her infidelities and coarseness? Pepys, probably, or Evelyn. If kings could suffer from whatever it was, Antonia thought hollowly, perhaps she shouldn't feel quite so shattered by her own weakness.

Last night Philip had been every woman's fantasy of the dream lover, at once tender and masterful, giving her as much pleasure as he got, sating her with rapture until she had no hook on to real life, could feel nothing but the exquisite sensations he produced.

And then, after her lies, he had become another fantasy, a man who took what he wanted. Oh, she had resisted—for shamefully few seconds, but inevitably she had surrendered to that fantasy, too. If he had intended to be cruel he hadn't succeeded. They had made love with all the fire and ecstasy of passionate lovers, losing themselves so that she had gone to sleep in his arms, forgetting that he had only wanted her for ulterior reasons, that he was no better than Bryan. Just more subtle, and more experienced, and more cruel. Both men had used her. Bryan had made her pregnant; Philip could have, too.

She shuddered, one hand reaching slowly for her midriff. Would she never learn?

Oddly enough, it was the thought that those companionable hours with him had been mere acting on his part that hurt the most. Sexual betrayal was bitter, but this was a violation of her heart and mind.

That was why she felt so dazed and bewildered. Philip's treachery, she thought wearily, visualising a world drained of colour and action, would mark her for life. As though this daunting conclusion was too much for her to cope with at the moment, she sank into the sleep denied her the night before.

The day drifted by, snared by the sun, dreamy with the sound of soft waves and cicadas, grey with pain. Antonia set her delicate jaw and gritted her teeth and straightened the perfect cupid's bow of her mouth, and endeavoured to face it out.

But the depths of her anguish frightened her. She hadn't felt like this when Bryan told her just how she was going to fit into his life, nor when she lost the baby.

That night she didn't sleep at all, and she left the bach in the grey light of dawn, unable to stay any longer. Away from it she might be able to erase the bitter memories and learn to face the future with her head held high. She had done it once before; she could do it again.

Once home she looked painfully around. Warm autumn rains had sent every weed seed growing, and the normally pristine beds around the courtyard had a shaggy, undisciplined look that was completely at variance with the carefully cultivated air of informality she liked. Not for the first time she recalled those gardens that spread around Motupipi, such a magnificent framework for a real gardener to get her hands on to.

Well, she couldn't do anything about them, but she could exhaust herself working in her small plot, and then perhaps she might be able to sleep at night. But before starting she needed to unpack and wash, and get some milk.

An hour later she sat down with a cup of tea and the newspaper, determined to plough her way through a salutary dose of the world's woes. Misery loves company, she thought grimly.

Almost the first thing she saw was a photograph of Philip with Laurie Preece, both clearly enjoying each other's company at a reception given by the mayor for a visiting company. On her engagement finger Laurie Preece wore a ring with a large, coloured stone.

Jealousy, corrosive as acid, seared through Antonia. *I can't bear it,* she thought. Oh, God, I can't bear it.

Tears ached behind her eyes, but she blinked them back. Swiftly she turned to the business section. Yet even there she couldn't escape; her dazed eyes fell on a nauseatingly coy little article headed 'A Possible Merger?' There were rumours, the reporter chattily informed her and anyone else interested, that the two old-established conglomerates of Preece and Angove were thinking of a merger, but not in the business sense. No, it was the scion of each family, the beauteous and very successful Laurie and the shrewd, clear-thinking Philip who were rumoured to be engaged. Neither side would confirm or deny it, although Miss Preece was wearing an emerald ring on her engagement finger; Philip Angove couldn't be contacted, but George Preece had laughed and said that he certainly wasn't going to pre-empt anything at this time.

Cold dread iced through Antonia's stomach, pooling at the base of her spine.

No, she thought, getting to her feet. No and no and no. She wasn't going to let herself be tormented by newspaper photographs and gossip. Philip had betrayed her in the most hurtful way possible, but he was not going to ruin her life.

On Monday Heather was full of news. She had spent the weekend at home where, so she said, it was already common knowledge that the engagement was to be announced soon.

'Laurie spent the weekend there,' she said happily. 'Isn't she absolutely exquisite? I'll bet they have the most enormous wedding.' Her voice dropped. 'It'll have to be soon, though, so Mrs Angove can go. She's very ill, you know. Mum says she hasn't got much longer.'

Antonia gave her a horrified look. Was this true, or mere ghoulish speculation? Surely Philip would have told her—he had said something about worrying his mother into an early grave, but that had been a figure of speech. Hadn't it? Perhaps she could ask Tiffany, although she hated the thought of seeming to pry.

'Haven't you got an interview in the wilds of the North Shore?' she asked Heather, desperate to change the subject.

'Yes, but it's all right, I've got plenty of time to get there. I'll see you about midday.'

Antonia sat down, her fingers slowly unclenching. Beads of moisture sprang out at her temples and on her top lip. Her head had been aching since she woke up, but it had begun to thump unmercifully. Shivering now that her anger had faded to a bleak bitterness, she walked across to the window, and stood staring down the light-well with eyes that saw nothing. So Laurie Preece had spent the weekend at Motupipi; it seemed as though the newspaper had got it right.

She reached for the telephone, but snatched her hand back. She simply could not ring Tiffany and ask her whether Mrs Angove was dying.

Somehow Antonia managed to get through the rest of the afternoon, but once home she went out into the green haven of her courtyard and collapsed into the lounger beneath the Australian frangipani.

She couldn't summon the energy to garden. The passion that had always given her solace failed her now. Her throat ached in concert with her head, but she refused to give in to her emotions.

Everyone, she tried to convince herself, was entitled to make a mistake now and then. Bryan had been her

first, Philip Angove was going to be her last. She just
had to put the whole shaming business behind her. After
all, it wasn't as though she was ever going to meet him
again. And she hadn't been a sensitive, blushing virgin
who had been seduced by a man who thought nothing
of her innocence, as she had been the first time; the affair
with Bryan had made her an experienced woman.

An experienced woman who hadn't even bothered to
make sure that she was protected! But then, Philip, who
was probably even more experienced than she was, hadn't
done anything about it either. A curious, elemental satisfaction spread through her. She would have been pre-
pared to swear on oath that the cool, logical man with
whom she had discussed the world and its affairs was
too rational to lose all reason and self-discipline, yet he
had been just as heedless, just as carried away by hunger
and passion as she had.

It was a small comfort in a world suddenly grown dark.

This anguish gave him far too much importance, too
much prominence. He was nothing but a con man, an
opportunist who had preyed on her weakness for men
with money and social position. Eventually she'd forget
him.

But if his mother really was dying—no, not even that
could excuse his behaviour!

As she stood staring around her garden in the sultry
dusk, she wondered how long it was going to take to
pick up the threads of her serenity again. Stifling a chill
that emanated from her bones, she went inside to pick
at a salad.

When the telephone rang she had just accepted that
the aching head and strained throat she'd been suffering
from for the last three days were not so much indi-
cations of her need to weep as symptoms of some sort
of infection.

It was Philip. 'You're needed here at Motupipi,' he
said curtly.

Shock froze the words in her mouth. She had to swallow harshly before she could answer. 'You must be mad.'

There was a pause, until he said in a voice hard enough to crack iron, 'Either you come up, Antonia, or I'll come down to get you.'

She should keep quiet, she knew she should, but her anger was so intense that it would have killed her to stay silent. 'I'm not going to destroy that tape, not now, not ever.'

Something in his voice altered; it became cold and slow and savage. 'You knew, didn't you? Right from the start, I suppose. You had your revenge handed to you on a plate,' he said. 'Damn you, you lying, conniving little bitch, you could have told me.'

Antonia pulled the receiver away from her ear and stared at it with total bewilderment, then put it slowly down. When it rang again almost immediately she backed away as though it had gone mad. It continued to demand attention for several minutes until at last it fell silent. Slowly, her head throbbing with painful monotony, she swallowed two aspirins before crawling into bed.

An hour later her stuporous sleep was interrupted by an urgent, imperative thundering on her door. Bewildered, she sat up, pushing hot strands of hair back from her temples. Her mouth was dry and her throat sore, and her eyes were hot, but at least the aspirins had got rid of most of the headache. Shakily she made her way down the passage and came to a stop behind the door.

'Who is it?' Her voice was croaky and uneven.

'Philip.'

When she hesitated he said distinctly, 'I'll break the door down if you don't open it.'

The virus must have weakened her resistance for she turned the key in the deadlock. He loomed against the glow of the street lamps, tall and dark and fiercely determined, his face all angles and planes.

'What do you want?' she asked, blocking the doorway.

'My mother wants to see you.'

Stupid, frantic tears sprang to her eyes. Swallowing fiercely, she said, 'Oh, God, is there nothing you won't try? Once and for all, I'm not going to destroy that tape.' She tried to slam the door shut, but he pushed it open and forced her back, his expression coldly inimical.

'And I'm not going to stand here arguing,' he said, each word bitten off as though he had reached the end of his tether. 'Get into some clothes and come with me, for God's sake! I've had to leave my mother's deathbed because you wouldn't bloody well forget your grievance for long enough to feel some sort of compassion for her.'

Appalled, Antonia stared at him, but her head was thick and woolly, and she couldn't think. 'I'm sorry,' she said, one hand massaging the back of her neck. 'I didn't know, Philip.'

His voice cracked like a whip. 'What's the matter with you?'

'I think I'm getting flu,' she said, her lack-lustre voice more convincing than she realised.

'God, will nothing go right?' His fists clenched at his sides. The ferocity in his tone made her flinch. Very slightly the fierce, hawk-like regard softened. He put his hand on her shoulder and pushed her gently back into the passage. 'Antonia, you have to come with me. She wants to see you.'

The stiff rigidity of her face melted into compassion; without even thinking she stepped forward and hugged him.

For a moment he relaxed, resting his cheek on the top of her head, but almost immediately he pushed her away. 'Get dressed,' he said, 'and bring whatever medication you've been taking with you. And please, Antonia, hurry!'

'I'm sorry,' she said, painful tears at the back of her eyes as she hurried into her bedroom. 'Why didn't you tell me?'

'Because first you hung up on me, and then you wouldn't answer. I tried the Buchanans; I thought you would listen to Tiffany, but their nanny said they're not at home. She refused to tell me where they are. It doesn't matter—just get going.'

In spite of his steady tone she could hear the tension and the anguish in his words.

'They're spending the night in Auckland,' she said dully as she pulled on trousers in a fanciful tweed of blue and navy and lemon.

He waited outside as she struggled into a shirt and a woollen jersey in her favourite iced lemon, and slid a packet of aspirin into her bag, then ran a brush through her hair.

'You'll need a jacket,' he said from the doorway.

Keeping her eyes averted, she hauled one from the wardrobe and slung it over her shoulder. 'I'm ready,' she said huskily.

He drove very fast all the way up to Motupipi while Antonia dozed uneasily, waking to a disconnected, frightened feeling, as though she had been snatched from her own life and forced to participate in another's. She didn't try to work out what she'd say when Mrs Angove asked her to destroy that wretched tape. Her brain seemed to have turned into mush, and although she was acutely conscious of Philip's presence beside her she couldn't feel anything more for him than a vast sympathy.

She should hate him for what he had done to her, but at the moment all she could think of was that he was hurting, and that there was nothing she could do about it, no way she could ease his pain.

She understood now why he had betrayed her. His mother was dying, and he loved her. Of course he would go to almost any extreme to make her happy.

They arrived at Motupipi shortly after midnight, and were met by Brenda, her normally cheerful face drawn with worry and grief.

'How is she?' Philip's voice was deep and harsh and brusque.

'Holding on.' Brenda took Antonia's bag from his hand and said, 'I'll put this in Antonia's bedroom. Go straight on down.'

Antonia couldn't help herself. She curled her small hand around Philip's, gripping tightly. After a moment his fingers relaxed, and fastened around hers, and together they walked down towards Mrs Angove's apartments.

It hadn't been much more than a month since Antonia had seen her last, but she was shocked by the difference. A nurse got up from her chair on the other side and looked steadily at Philip. She gave a tiny shake of her head before walking silently into the next room.

'I'm so sorry,' Mrs Angove whispered as Antonia came up to her, 'but I really needed to say this to you. I've already told Philip. I wanted him to make you stop that tape, and I'm afraid I did all the awful feminine things which our mothers told us were the way you managed a man, but which you young things despise so rightly. I cried and pleaded and said that it made me bitterly unhappy.'

'It doesn't matter,' Antonia said, her mind made up.

'Yes, it does. It made things so difficult—Philip knew I was trying to manipulate him, of course, but he's always been very protective of me.'

'Mrs Angove, you don't have to ask me. I'll edit the tape.'

Philip's hand clenched so tightly on hers that she gave a faint gasp. But his mother was shaking her head. 'No. Because it's all true.'

'True?' Antonia had wondered, of course. Mrs Angove's desperation had been suspicious. Even so, to have her faint suspicions confirmed made her head reel.

A slight smile pulled at the older woman's bloodless lips. 'Yes, and I don't regret it, not a bit. I do regret going back to John, but Edward had left me, he was so horrified by poor Kate's death, and—I wanted my baby to grow up at Motupipi. I knew there couldn't be any children for John, you see, and so did he, which was the only reason he took me back. The last Angove. The heir. Family means so much to the Angoves. He never forgave me, never forgave Philip...'

She appeared to be rambling, the words tumbling fast and slurred, but when Philip said softly, 'It doesn't matter, darling. Don't worry about it any more,' she smiled.

'I'm sorry I didn't tell you,' she whispered. 'John made me promise, and we were taught to keep our promises...I'd broken so many...'

'It's all right,' he repeated, his voice very gentle as he took her hand and held it.

She looked past him to Antonia, hovering by the bed and awkwardly wondering whether she should leave, 'I'm sorry, I made things difficult for——'

Antonia said quietly but in her most definite tone, 'Mrs Angove, I promise you everything is all right now. Please don't worry about it any more.'

The green eyes, as brilliant as her son's but without the tracery of gold, held Antonia's for a long second. Then the woman in the bed sighed and smiled. 'You have grace of soul,' she breathed. 'Thank you.'

Antonia left them then, to walk slowly back down the wide corridor, lapped by some sort of peace. Poor Mrs Angove, loving one man and married to another, forced to watch as he withheld his affection from the boy he called his son. And poor Philip, a sacrifice to the altar of family heritage. She understood him much better now, understood why he had tried so hard to seduce her acquiescence, why he was marrying Laurie Preece, who was so entirely suitable. When you had been brought up to believe that the family was all-important, it tended to warp your appreciation of right and wrong, honour and dishonour.

Brenda met her at the front door. 'Where do you think you're going?' she asked. 'You look awful.'

'Thanks.' Suddenly Antonia realised that her head was banging and her nose and eyes were stuffed up; she could hardly bear to swallow, and she felt as though someone were directing a hot fan at her. In spite of that, she was shivering. 'I can't stay here,' she said vaguely. 'I have to get home.'

'You can't go home like that. You're sick. Come on, into bed with you.'

Brenda was adamant, overruling Antonia's feeble protests. Before very long she was lying naked between the sheets in the room she thought of as hers, staggering off to sleep. She woke several times, once to a man who examined her with the professional impersonality that marked him as a doctor, and said that she had a virus, but she'd live.

'I know that,' she croaked crossly, and he gave her a somewhat harried grin and said, 'Take these pills and drink plenty of liquids——'

'I have to go back home.'

'Not for a couple of days, no.'

Her throat hurt but she said firmly, 'I can't stay here, they're in enough——'

'You're not going anywhere.' It was Philip's voice, cold and decisive.

Frowning, she opened her eyes and scanned the room. All she could see was his black silhouette against the paler window. 'I have to go,' she explained hoarsely.

'You're staying. I'll ring Heather and tell her that you're ill.'

'Too much trouble,' she muttered.

'I'll decide that,' he returned implacably. 'Go back to sleep.'

When she awoke again the cool grey light of dawn was seeping into the room. For a moment she lay rigid in the big bed, wondering where on earth she was. Then she heard the softest of noises, the gentle hush of waves on some distant beach, and she realised that she was at Motupipi.

A cautious inventory revealed that she felt surprisingly well. It was too soon for antibiotics to have worked but the decongestants seemed to have done the trick, and although she certainly wasn't her normal self she no longer felt like the next best thing to a dishrag. Warily she turned her head, and discovered that the thudding had gone entirely.

She had to get out of there. Philip had got what he wanted from her; she was of no more use to him. Slowly she got up and washed, then dressed, not really sure what she would do, just intent on leaving the homestead before she saw him again.

Bag in hand, she was about to open the door when its silent swing inwards made her gasp. Philip came into the room. Antonia didn't have to ask whether his mother had died. His expression told her.

'Oh, Philip.' Her voice was thick and burdened by emotion.

'She died an hour ago,' he said flatly.

'I'm sorry.' Why weren't there more words, better words, to say what she felt? 'I'm sorry' sounded so bare, so emotionless.

'Are you?' He sounded like a savage, his voice honed to a weapon for striking and slashing to the bone. 'I doubt that; your intransigence almost certainly hastened her death.'

She drew in a harsh, painful breath. He was hurting, she realised numbly, and she was the only person he could take it out on. 'Nevertheless, I am sorry.'

'How sorry?'

She watched with dilated eyes as he looked around the tidy room. She had stripped and made the bed, bundling the linen into the clothes basket in the bathroom.

'Just as though you've never been here,' he said. The strong framework of his face was too prominent, the green-gold eyes those of a wild animal. 'I need comforting, Antonia. I need to forget my grief for a few minutes, and the sleek, hot sheath of your body would be the perfect way to do it. Will you comfort me now?'

And she almost reached for him, almost offered him the only solace she could—that of her body. Fortunately her innate sense of self-preservation jolted her into awareness of what she was about to do, and she froze.

'You don't know what you're asking.' Her voice dragged; she was so disgusted with herself that she couldn't even summon up the energy to give his suggestion the contempt it deserved.

'Why not? We were good, you and I, weren't we? You liked what we did together.'

'Philip, don't——'

'Don't what? Don't make waves? Just accept that I've performed stud services and leave it at that?'

The words hit her like bullets, each nicely judged to wound as painfully as possible. She winced and he laughed, softly, a sound without humour.

'No, you don't like the truth. But that's what happened, you little cheat, with your mermaid's face and your smooth, slim body, offering all the delirious glamour of fairyland. It turns to ashes and dead leaves, that fool's gold, and now I know it.'

He ran a cool, insulting hand over her breasts, and to her horror she felt the sudden tightness of arousal, the swift piercing sensations running through her like arrows.

Philip laughed. 'Yes. Shall we make love again, Antonia, you beautiful, heartless little bitch?'

She stared at him with a stony visage, willing her expression not to reveal the pain, the humiliation, that rasped through her.

'No?' he said, taunting her with his disbelief. 'Perhaps it's just as well. When I look at you I see a woman with no compassion, no softness, just a hard set of ethics.'

When he had gone she looked out of the window at the uncaring day and wept, the silent tears running down her face.

CHAPTER NINE

BAG in hand, Antonia went into the huge, modern kitchen, a chef's dream come true, and said to a red-eyed Brenda, 'I have to go home.'

Brenda gave her a harried look, but nodded. 'Yes, of course,' she said, 'but how? There's no bus, and——'

'I'll get a friend to come and pick me up.' Tiffany wouldn't mind, and, even if she did, this was an emergency. She couldn't stay here.

'Well, that would probably be the best thing,' Brenda said, but she looked worried. 'I wonder—Philip brought you up, didn't he? Perhaps he's got a way to——'

'He's bound to be busy.' Any huskiness in her voice would be put down to the virus. 'Don't interrupt him.'

Instead of the farm she rang the Buchanans' apartment in town, sighing with relief when Tiffany answered. 'I'm at Motupipi,' she said without preamble. 'Can you come and get me?'

Tiffany, bless her, turned up trumps. She didn't even ask what was going on, not when she arrived at Motupipi, nor afterwards, although she was clearly dying to know. She did suggest Antonia come home with her to the farm. Antonia began to say no, then suddenly realised that as Philip had been told the Buchanans were away he would never think of looking for her there. Not that he'd look, she thought drearily, swamped for a moment in the worst sort of self-pity, but just in case he did...

'If it's no trouble,' she said bleakly.

Tiffany snorted.

Once at the house she bustled Antonia into bed, made a hot lemon drink mixed under Eliot's supervision with a large slosh of brandy, gave her two more aspirins and a box of tissues, and told her not to even think of getting up for the rest of the day.

Friendship, Antonia thought just before she slid into oblivion, was much better for you than love.

It took her three days to get rid of the infection, three days when she felt like death, but the basic resilience of her immune system soon reasserted itself and by the end of the week she was well enough to go back to Auckland and work.

Unhappiness raged like a black beast at the bottom of her heart, but she was able to keep it caged most of the time. It snared perilously close to the surface when Heather told her about Mrs Angove's funeral, to attend which she had taken half a day off.

'It must have been quite an occasion.' Antonia cut off her rapturous description of Laurie Preece's outfit and demeanour abruptly. 'Now shall we get back to work?'

'Yes, of course.' Heather looked wounded, as well she might, Antonia thought grimly, compelled by guilt to be especially kind to her for the rest of the week.

The slow weeks dragged by. Antonia worked in her garden and did the things she usually did, went to the theatre with friends, dined out ditto, visited Tiffany and Eliot, saw whichever films appealed—to all intents and purposes her life carried on just the same.

But beneath the activity her emotions were enclosed in a dark vacuum of grief that sapped her energy and robbed her life of colour. She longed for Philip with a desperation amounting almost to obsession. She saw his face in her dreams, in her fantasies, she felt his touch, she even tasted the flavour of his skin, that salty masculine essence of virility—addictive, unforgettable.

Common sense told her it was because she had shut herself away from men, refusing to let herself fall in love again, so she had no experience beyond Bryan. Intellectually she accepted that familiarity would have eventually sated her hunger; instinct told her that she would always react to Philip with the wildfire magic that scorched through her even now when she thought of him. It was beyond desire, beyond need. Unfortunately for her, she had fallen in love with him, and love made its own rules, took no notice of reason and prudence and common sense.

Not that this turbulence of spirit and flesh and mind was her ideal of love. She had longed for a love that was security and contentment and the golden glow of happiness, a bond of liking and commitment and respect all bound up with desire, not this perilous pagan sorcery where reason and logic went out the window and the only moment to live for was the present.

She found herself wondering what Philip would think about things, arguing with him in her mind, examining her own reactions with the same incisive rigour he had used, and she missed him with an aching, bone-deep hunger that nothing seemed to overcome.

It was humiliating that she should love a man who thought nothing of using her helpless response to his dark male virility to persuade her into betraying her principles, even though it was for his mother's peace of mind. It was more humiliating that it was Philip who had taught her that making love could be as fiercely beautiful and overwhelming as the hiss of fire in a volcano's throat.

Disillusion should have sickened her. Instead it had clothed her imaginings in the violent hues of passion. Now she longed for him, missed him so much that it was eating away at her whole life, draining it of joy.

About a fortnight after Mrs Angove's death she discovered that there would be no baby. At first she was relieved, but in bed that night she found herself weeping into her pillow with such anguish that for far too long she couldn't control her grief.

Eventually she staggered up to get a glass of water, avoiding the sight of her swollen reflection in the mirror. Her grief horrified her. Of course she was precariously poised, her emotions abraded raw, her whole being tight with tension, but the storm of weeping had been unlike her. Usually she was able to control herself.

That night she dreamed about her baby, the one she had lost, the child she and Bryan had made the night he seduced her. Although she had miscarried too early to know what sex it was, it had always appeared in her dreams as a laughing little girl, sitting in a field of flowers with other children. In the manner of dreams the images flowed and coalesced into each other, and she wasn't surprised when at last the baby held out its arms. Always before this had been the moment, when she was reaching for her child, that some inexorable fate had snatched it sobbing from her grasp, leaving her bereft in a world gone dark with menace.

This time in the dream Antonia kissed the baby and watched, waving happily, as the flowery meadow lifted and flew serenely into the sky.

It didn't take Freud to discern the meaning of the dream. Relinquishment. But why now, after all these years?

Slowly, lying in her bed in the darkness, she began to see a pattern. She had never been able to mourn the child; her anguish at its loss had been merely a part of the greater anguish of betrayal. It hadn't just been Bryan's callous treatment of her that had kept her behind the barricades of her heart all these years.

The defection of her father and the subsequent decline of her mother into alcoholism and promiscuity had made her need for love and respect stronger even than the push of her hormones and her vanity. That was why Bryan had found her such easy prey. She longed for the family she had lost, desperately wanting to be loved. And that was why she had been so shattered when it all blew up in her face; she had failed to satisfy any of her needs, and lost the child as well.

She had blamed Bryan, but really her decision never to fall in love again had been based on the hidden fear that to surrender to her own sexuality meant to risk the loss of any child she might have.

Last night's dream seemed to indicate that at last she had overcome the fear; the question was, how? The only thing she had done, she thought grimly, was fall in love once more with a man almost as deceitful as Bryan. Not quite, however. Philip had, after all, made no promises. He hadn't even seduced her, unless it was with his mind and his conversation; she had known exactly why he had been seeing her when they made love.

But he had used her.

Yet now she understood his reasons she could almost forgive him. He loved his mother.

What was hurting so much was that after their night together, a night that had been the acme of her existence, he had left her. He hadn't even contacted her to see whether he had made her pregnant. His behaviour brutally reinforced her knowledge that she had merely been a means to an end.

Well, she wasn't going to let it blight her life; it hurt, but she was stronger now than she had been when she was eighteen.

And there was no baby to complicate things.

No doubt Philip would end up married to Laurie Preece. After all, she was *suitable*. She had *breeding*.

Tears welled up again but Antonia swallowed them back. She was far from the first woman to have fallen in love and made a fool of herself.

But she missed Philip. With slow acceptance, she admitted that his absence left a great, gaping hole in the fabric of her life. Such dark magic he had used against her; it was part of its strength that even though she knew it was bad for her she craved it still. As well as the blazing physical attraction there had been a rare communion of minds.

And, damn it, he had enjoyed her company, too! He had liked matching wits with her, enjoyed the evenings when they talked about almost every subject under the sun. She was astute enough to have seen through any attempts to fake it.

The knowledge was something to bolster her wounded spirit.

That night marked a turning-point. Antonia decided to make plans for her future, and spent a whole weekend writing down a series of goals, none of which, she realised as she looked down at them, she particularly wanted to achieve.

Her pointed chin jutted at a dangerous angle. Well, she would force herself to become interested in them. Philip Angove was not going to turn the rest of her life into a desert. The men in his family seemed rather too good at doing that—witness Edward, who had seduced his brother's wife and got her with child, then run away, leaving her to the mercy of her husband, a callous, un-loving tyrant.

They were a dangerous crew, the Angove men. Philip was a fitting heir to that tainted legacy.

The letter came the next day. Mrs Angove had left her something in her will. It would be convenient if she picked it up at Motupipi the following Saturday at two in the afternoon.

About as impersonal as an iceberg, and as cold. Antonia's eyes traced the slashing black signature, very striking and confident, and legible, too. Something died within her, something she thought had died long ago.

Without thinking she sat down and wrote back, saying that it wasn't convenient for her to call at Motupipi. She would always remember his mother's kindness to her, and that was the only memento she needed to mark their association.

Go to hell, she thought with grim satisfaction as she put it with the others to be posted.

It was odd, she thought a week later as she riffled through her private mail, that hope could die so many deaths. Of course she had been waiting for a reply;

perhaps she had even made that letter deliberately provocative in the hope of inciting one, but none had come.

She looked around the small sitting-room, and said aloud, 'This is the end. This is it, finally, once and for all. From now on I'm going to forget that he ever existed.'

Sheer will-power and a dogged refusal to give in to self-pity weren't exactly comfortable, but they helped get you over the worst bits of your life.

The next evening she went to a poetry reading in a pub with a group of friends from her university days, arriving home around eleven, her spirits higher than they had been since—for months, she substituted. Usually she left a light on in the sitting-room, but as she had gone straight from work the whole house was in darkness. She drove into her small carport and got out, hurrying a little as she always did. She wasn't afraid, but she was careful.

'About bloody time you got home,' a masculine voice said, an icy control reinforcing the savage timbre.

Gasping, she whirled to face him, clenching her car keys in her fingers to make a serviceable knuckle-duster. For a moment fear overlaid the primitive joy. Then she relaxed, striving desperately to call on her composure.

'What are you doing here?' Her voice was thin and shaken.

'I came,' he said with a silky urbanity that somehow frightened her more than anything else, 'to give you the bequest my mother made.'

She drew a deep breath and held out her hand. 'It wasn't necessary for you to bring it personally, but very well, you can give it to me now.'

There was a flash of white in the darkness as he took her hand. His fingers closed around her wrist, not painfully but with a decision that made it clear she was his prisoner until he chose to let her go. 'Open the door and invite me inside,' he commanded.

Her heart twisted painfully. 'I don't want you inside,' she said, gritting her teeth to hide the tremor in her voice.

'Too bad.' He picked her up and carried her to the door, where he calmly appropriated the keys and opened her door.

Antonia held herself rigid, because every bone and sinew and cell in her body wanted to relax into that hard, binding embrace. She was seething with rage and frustration when he set her down on her feet, but she managed to contain her emotions. It was the only way to deal with him.

'Now that you've shown me how macho you can be,' she bit out, 'finish your business and go.'

He locked the door and pocketed the keys, so that she was to all intents and purposes caged in her own house. Turning, he smiled down into her small set face and said smoothly, 'Don't give me orders, you little termagant.'

She drew another breath and he bent and kissed her expertly on the mouth, stifling the hot words with casual, insulting ease. It was useless to struggle, and undignified, so Antonia stayed lax in his arms, refusing to respond as his mouth hardened into a savage demand. Only when it was over and he was watching her from narrowed eyes did she show any signs of response.

'I can't beat you when it comes to strength,' she said frigidly.

'Oh, I don't know. As far as strength of will is concerned you're more than a match for me.'

'Does Laurie Preece know you're here?'

He shrugged, an ironic smile not softening the severe contours of his mouth. 'I doubt it, but then this has nothing to do with Laurie. And before we go any further, let's clear one thing up. I am not engaged to her, never have been, and have absolutely no intention of marrying her. Ever.'

It was impossible to doubt him. Antonia schooled her face to reveal nothing of the relief and elation that swamped her, for, after all, what difference did it make? It had been two months since his mother died, and in that time he hadn't come near her. He could not love her, even if he didn't love Laurie.

'But she was just an excuse, wasn't she?' he said, his lashes drooping. 'You must have known damned well that there was nothing between us.'

'It was rumoured that you were going to get engaged,' she said steadily, 'and Heather seemed to think it was a foregone conclusion. And she wore an engagement ring in the newspaper photograph.'

'Just a ring,' he corrected. 'Her father is ridiculously indulgent, so she has more jewellery than is good for her.'

She shrugged. 'It doesn't matter.'

'No?' His eyes mocked her. He gave her a gentle push. 'Into the sitting-room. I'm not going to talk to you here.'

'We have nothing to talk about,' she snapped, feeling herself inexorably backed into the room. Her expression was stony, her voice as cold and brittle as an Antarctic ice river.

'Don't be an idiot.'

His curt reply effectively reduced her to silence, but she refused to sit down and stood defiantly in the middle of her pretty room, staring at him with unconcealed belligerence. He looked as assured as he always did, glossy with the patrician patina of wealth and confidence and authority, but she sensed a new hardness about him, as though he had reinforced his formidable will with steel.

Antonia lifted her chin. Her eyes dared him to convince her of anything.

'Laurie is spoilt,' he said, his eyes never leaving her face, 'and accustomed to getting her own way. Her mother was a great friend of my mother's, and they hatched this scheme of us marrying when Laurie was just a kid. My mother was sensible enough not to tell me, and these past few years she'd given up on the idea completely, but Mrs Preece seems to have brought Laurie up on the belief that she and I are soulmates. I think she really believed that eventually, when she'd stopped having a good time, we'd settle down and marry. She knows better now. As soon as the rumours surfaced in the newspaper I told her and her family that I had no plans to marry her.'

Antonia's hands were tightly held by her sides. He was so close she could see the faint pulse beating in his throat, the small fan of lines at the corner of each eye.

'Why are you bothering to tell me this?' she asked hoarsely. 'It makes no difference to me——'

'Just listen,' he commanded. 'Laurie wasn't the real problem, was she?' He paused, waiting for her to say something, but Antonia couldn't have spoken if she'd wanted to. He resumed, 'The real problem was my mother's determination to get rid of that tape, and your firm conviction that I'd planned to seduce you into doing it.'

'You more or less admitted it,' she said fiercely. 'Except that I seduced you first.'

He showed his teeth in a smile that held no humour. 'I doubt whether either of us had the edge. We were both reckless enough that night to take anything we could get. It was the most exciting experience of my life, and it was fundamentally flawed. I knew that even as I took you, but when you told me that that was all you wanted from me——' His hands tightened into fists. After a moment he went on tonelessly. 'I don't think I've ever come so close to killing anyone as I did then.'

'Instead, you made love to me again.'

'It started as a punishment,' he confessed, 'but it didn't stay that way. With you I have no control—I think that's why I was so brutal. It's never happened to me like that before. But I didn't come up to Whangaroa to seduce you into editing that bloody tape.'

She said heavily, 'It doesn't matter——'

'Some day you'll tell me why you were so suspicious, so ready to believe the worst of me,' he interrupted in a hard voice. 'Because although I was clumsy that night at Whangaroa—well, it was only two days after my

mother had told me that the doctors gave her no hope
of recovery, and I was still in shock. Yes, I was going
to *ask* you to edit that bloody tape, but the reason I
followed you up there was because I'd missed you so
much. And the reason I was so cruel was that I resented
what I thought to be some kind of addiction. Although
I wanted you just this side of madness, I was happy just
to sit with you and talk to you, hear you laugh, match
wits with you. It had never happened like that with me
before. Your absence made me hungry. I wanted to get
the business of the tape out of the way before we made
love.' He watched her from half-closed eyes. 'If I'd told
you how ill she was, Antonia, what would you have
said?'

'That's not fair.' He said nothing, and after a moment
she sighed. Something hard and unregenerate inside her
was soothed by his presence. 'I suppose I'd have said
what I did when—the night she died.'

A muscle jumped in his jaw. 'Instead, you seduced
me, then told me scornfully that you didn't need me, or
any other man, that all you wanted from me was my
body.'

She said on a sad little laugh, 'You're not the only
one with pride, you know.'

'No.' He took a deep breath, releasing it slowly. He
hadn't been looking at her; now he walked across and
looked out through the uncurtained window to the
courtyard. 'So I went back,' he said in a remote voice,
'and my mother was visibly losing ground, still fretting.
I hated you for making me want you, and I hated that
flinty integrity that stopped you from giving in, even
though I knew I was asking you to betray everything you
believed in.'

'It wasn't only that,' she said, holding on to her composure with difficulty. 'It was Mrs Collins, too. She
wanted Kate's name remembered. I *couldn't* just wipe
it like that.'

'I had no right to try and force you to.' He swung around, his face dark with suppressed emotion. 'I wanted some sort of symbolic surrender. You say you have pride—well, I was brought up to be proud, to think that as an Angove I was the heir to traditions and a heritage or some importance. But by then I knew that if you wanted to you could bring me to my knees. I discovered that the night we almost made love here, on this sofa, and I heard myself promising you anything you wanted. I could have stayed that night, I intended to, but—I suppose you could say I ran away. I despised myself, and I resented you.'

Antonia didn't know what to say, although his explanation was making too much sense. Of course he would despise himself for lusting after a woman who wasn't suitable, who was a nobody, especially if he thought this gave her power over him.

'So it was doubly ironic,' he said between his teeth, 'that what was worrying my mother was how to tell me that I wasn't my father's son, but his nephew, the child of an adulterous interlude with his brother. My sweet, charming mother had a violent affair with her husband's brother, who happened to be engaged to one of her best friends. She conceived a child to him, and then he, one of the proud Angoves, ran away and left her to a life of misery with his brother. When she told me I felt sick, and betrayed, and bitter.'

This was a reaction Antonia hadn't expected. She breathed, 'Philip—don't.' and went to him, sliding her arms around him in a purely instinctive gesture.

His arms closed compulsively about her. For a long moment they stood locked together, both giving and accepting comfort, but just before she started to feel uneasy he released her, saying in a hard voice, 'I had to pretend that it was all right, that I wasn't upset, when all the time I thought their sleazy, cowardly affair had all but ruined any hopes I might have had with you. And my pride and arrogance had made the whole situation infinitely worse.'

'They were not sleazy or cowardly,' she said unevenly. 'At least, your mother wasn't.'

His mouth twisted in a humourless smile. 'Exactly. The true Angoves didn't come out of the situation well at all.'

She said diffidently, 'He—John—must have thought of you as his son. In all the ways there are, you were his son.'

He said harshly, 'He hated my guts from the time I was a baby, just as he hated my mother. But he was an Angove, and Angoves need heirs, and Angoves don't make scandals. Do you know how much of a sacrifice he demanded of my mother, of me? Apparently he blackmailed Edward, who was a diplomat, with the threat of exposure, which would have put paid to his career. And he told my mother that if she didn't live with him as his wife he would wait until her child was born and take it from her and bring it up himself.'

'Oh, no!'

'So she gave in,' he said savagely. 'And she paid for that security with years of his cold, complete contempt. His arrogant insistence on his Angove pride cost me my childhood and my mother her pride, her happiness, everything. She had given in to an overwhelming desire, and the only result was tragedy.'

He wasn't asking for sympathy; there was terrible anger in his voice, not pain. Antonia said quietly, 'Your father—I mean John Angove—must have suffered, too.'

'You'd never have known,' he said quietly. 'He was stone all the way through. Oddly enough, it was only when I finally gave up trying to impress him, when I was seventeen or so, that he showed any signs of respecting me.'

'He must have been so bitter.' Antonia thought she could understand some small part of John Angove's anguish. 'After all, he had been betrayed in the most basic way.'

'You're too forgiving. I doubt whether I'll ever forget their shabby conniving, let alone forgive it.'

'Why? Surely your mother paid enough——'

'Because I'm subject to the same sort of lust that drove my mother and Edward into each other's arms.'

Pain speared through her as her eyes searched the dark mask of his face. Unbidden words trembled on her tongue, but instinct warned her to keep silent.

'I raped you,' he said.

'No,' she whispered, shocked. 'It wasn't rape. I could have stopped you.'

His mouth twisted again. 'Could you?'

She said more firmly, 'Yes! Anyway, it's not relevant, because I wanted it as much as you did.'

'And that was all you wanted from me.' His smile was mirthless, edged with anger. 'You could say it was natural justice, or you could say I was hoist with my own petard, if you have a taste for clichés. Because by the time I got home I knew I'd made the biggest mistake in my life.'

Hope struck a faint, flickering glow on her heart. He was looking at her with bleak, desolate eyes, his gaze searching her face as though he was trying to imprint her features on his memory strongly enough to last him for the rest of his life.

Uneasily, wondering whether his mother's revelations had persuaded him to do the honourable thing, she said, 'I think you should try to forgive your father, and your mother. Bitterness is not worth it. Believe me, I know.'

'I don't blame you for not wanting to get any further involved,' he said stiffly. 'An unsavoury business, all in all. Betrayal all round—and the worst was my betrayal of you, because you were a completely innocent party.'

'It depends entirely on what you see as betrayal,' she said slowly. She didn't know how to deal with this. 'I knew, you see. You didn't make me any promises, except that you'd hunt me down. I knew you wanted to persuade me to change my mind. I let myself——'

She stopped. She had almost said, I let myself love you. And, although hope was being reborn in her heart, she couldn't surrender to it. He was explaining, but he hadn't said that he loved her. Wanted, yes, but he wasn't like Bryan, he didn't use the easy lies.

'When I asked you to edit the tape,' he said slowly, watching her, 'you seemed to have been expecting it. What made you assume that I had only wanted you for that?'

She looked at him with veiled eyes, and thought, Why not? He was being open; she could reciprocate. 'When I was eighteen I fell in love with a man who thought I was like my mother.'

'What was your mother like? You said she was a nurse.'

It was surprising that he remembered. 'Yes. A good nurse, until the wine got to her. As well as alcohol my mother took up men after my father left us.' She gave a painful smile. 'She was looking for love, I suppose. Or forgetfulness, or comfort.'

'No wonder you turned me down after Mother died.' He gave her a look in which pain and disgust were equally mingled. 'I bitterly regret that. I behaved appallingly, said the most atrocious things to you, and the only excuse I've got is that I knew you were backing off, I knew that any hope we had of happiness was long gone, and that my actions were the cause of my unhappiness. One of these days I hope you might be able to forgive me.'

'I knew you were unhappy,' she said swiftly. 'You don't need my forgiveness, Philip.'

'No?' He waited, and when she remained silent said, 'Tell me about this lover of yours. You were lovers, I gather?'

'Couldn't you tell I wasn't a virgin?'

'By the time I got there,' he said slowly, watching her with half-closed eyes, 'I wouldn't have cared if you'd had a hundred men before me. I didn't want a virgin, I wanted you and you alone. But you were certainly tight and small enough to be as virginal as any man would want, if he was hung up on it.'

Colour flooded her cheeks. 'Yes, well, Bryan and I were lovers. I was too thick to know that a man from the West Coast equivalent of the gentry would want only one thing from me. Sex. He got it quite easily. I was besotted with him. I thought he was in love with me, and we'd get married, and life would be like a fairy-tale from then on.'

'And what happened?'

She smiled painfully. 'I got pregnant, probably the night he seduced me. When I told him he said it was tough, he was engaged to a girl from Nelson, and I'd better have an abortion, but there was no reason for me to worry about anything else, because he wasn't tired of me by a long way. The girl from Nelson was a much better match, she had *breeding* and *background* and money, she knew how to behave, she knew all the right people. But I had the sex appeal. He would look after me, set me up in a house, and I could keep my job at the office, and that way I'd always be ready for him. It would be an arrangement that would satisfy all of us, except perhaps his wife, and she wouldn't know anything about it.'

The imprecation was barely audible, but Antonia winced at the raw rage. His face was set in a cold, hard mask.

'So what happened then?'

'Oh, I behaved in a melodramatic fashion, running away into the rainy night. He couldn't find me, and I slipped and spent all night out in the rain, got a mild case of hypothermia and lost the baby, so he didn't have to pay for an abortion. But I refused to sleep with him again so he got me sacked. He had plenty of influence in the town; he was the biggest landowner, and his custom was valuable. It was easy enough to put a little pressure on. They didn't want to get rid of me, but——' she shrugged '—he was a lot more important than I ever would be.'

'No wonder you reacted so badly when I threatened you with sacking.'

'It made me profoundly suspicious of people with power,' she said tightly.

'What happened then?'

'I was living with Tiffany's parents at the time, and they were wonderful; they helped me decide what I wanted to do. I took my poor little broken heart off to university and vowed never to fall in love again. I'd convinced myself that I loved him, you see, and he'd told me he loved me.'

'I hope I never meet him,' he said harshly, 'because if I do I might well kill him.'

Sheer shock kept her silent. The black rage in his face made her shiver with fear. 'He wasn't very old,' she said quietly.

'Old enough to know better. No wonder you didn't trust me.'

'You never lied to me.'

'Only by implication.' There was silence until he said, 'I'm sorry. It's no recompense, but I'm sorry.'

'It's all right.' Her eyes burned with the effort of keeping tears back.

Then he said in quite a different voice, 'Damn it, that's not the way it's going to end! Look at me, Antonia!'

The quick, forceful command took her by surprise. Her eyes flashed upwards. He was looking at her with arrogant authority, a handsome buccaneer, resolute and implacable. He said curtly, 'You said that all you wanted was an affair. All right, we'll have an affair——'

'No!'

'—but I warn you, I don't intend to let it stop at that. I'll follow you to Christchurch if I have to, but sooner or later you'll accept that whatever you feel for me isn't just lust, it's more than that.'

'I'm not going to Christchurch,' she said. 'It was a lie to stop you from suggesting that I'd make a good mistress.'

'You must have been desperate, my poor little love. Are you going to forgive me, give me another chance?' His voice was persuasive, deep as the sea. He didn't attempt to touch her but she could feel him reach out to her, try to dominate her. She could have wept.

'I don't want an affair,' she said abruptly, afraid to hope, afraid to follow her heart. 'I'm not very good mistress material.'

'In that case,' he said coolly, 'we'd better get married.'

'Philip, don't.'

His determination, fierce and purposeful, beat against her frail defences. 'Don't what? Don't tell you that I love you? Don't ask you to try again?'

'You don't have to tell me you love me,' she said sadly. 'I know honour and the family name is important to the Angoves, but I'm not pregnant, you don't have to offer me marriage.'

His eyes glittered. 'Get this into your head,' he said. 'I am not your lover of nine years ago. I am glad you are not pregnant, but only because I don't want you to have even the slightest hint of doubt as to why I want to marry you. I waited these long months so that you'd know what your feelings for me were. I love you, and I want you, and if you don't agree I'll let you go, but I won't stop trying! Because I think you love me, too.'

'Don't you tell me how I feel,' she snapped, radiance lighting her from within. 'Of course I love you! I've loved you ever since we went out together that first time. But marriage—oh, God, what if you——?'

He sounded grim. 'How can I persuade you to trust me?'

She began to say something but he swept on, 'I never thought I'd say that, never mean it. I didn't believe love could exist. When I first saw you I was knocked right off my axis. And you seemed just as interested—you looked at me across that office and the air steamed up between us. But you were bloody obstinate, and I asked you up to Motupipi on an impulse. When you refused me I was intrigued, so I used a spot of mild blackmail to get you there.'

'Did you plan to leave it at that?'

He nodded. 'Yes. Oh, Mother had been fretting herself silly ever since Elva Collins rang up to tell her what she'd done, but I was sure she'd be quite happy with the restriction you suggested.'

'But she wasn't.'

He said soberly, 'No. So I asked you again to erase the tapes, and you refused. Please believe me, if you believe nothing else, as far as I was concerned that was it. Then I kissed you. You set me alight, damned near burned me out. I decided that it would be interesting to see what sort of person you were. I thought I'd be in complete control, that it was just sex.'

'And so it was,' she said wearily.

'No.' He shook his head, watching her with an expression of naked and passionate sincerity. 'I was playing a dangerous game, because every time I was with you I found myself becoming more and more fascinated until somewhere along the way fascination slipped into love. I just didn't recognise it. But I did know that I'd never met another woman who made me feel so alive, so open and whole and interested. Wanting you gnawed like a pain in my guts, but the need and the passion weren't everything; they weren't even the most important part of it.'

Antonia said quietly, 'I told myself that it was just that you were the most interesting man I'd ever met. You made me think and feel and hope again.'

'And then I blew it.' His voice was austere, almost flinty. He didn't wallow in recriminations, but she was learning to read him and behind the cold façade she recognised remorse and regret.

'We both blew it,' she said. 'I thought—I was so excited when you came to Whangaroa; I thought it meant
you loved me. I don't think I can tell you how I felt
when you—when you——'

'There's no excuse for the way I behaved, but the night
before Mother had been in pain, she'd cried, and I
thought of you, selfish, obstinate little bitch with your
diamond-hard ideas about ethics and standards.' He
shook his head. 'I came charging up there filled with
self-righteous indignation and desire and this hidden,
unrecognised love that I still persisted in thinking was
only lust. And we made love, and it shook the foundations of my world; it made me realise that whatever
I had done, whatever you had done, we were meant to
be together, two halves of the one whole.'

She said, 'I was afraid.' And honesty made her add,
'Philip, I'm still afraid.'

'I know. But Antonia, you can hold your own with
anyone; you have so much more to you than that sensual
appeal you despise. I love you more than I ever thought
I could love anyone else. I never thought that I'd need
a woman, but I need you. My life is flat and dreary, a
one-note symphony, without you. How can I make you
believe that?'

And she took the first step. 'You could hold me,' she
suggested, a smile beginning to break through. 'I think
I might begin to believe it if you held me.'

His laughter was exultant, triumphant, as was his
mouth when he finally kissed her. 'Darling,' he whispered. 'God, darling, I love you. Come home with me
to Motupipi and fill it full of flowers——'

Antonia's eyes widened. She had often thought that
he could read her mind but she had never really believed
it. Now she said, 'How did you know?'

He grinned. 'I saw your courtyard, the work of a gifted
gardener, and I saw the way you looked around the
grounds at home, mentally putting in flowers wherever
you looked.'

She tried to work out whether he wanted this. Still unsure of him, she said carefully, 'Would you mind?'

'Darling, you can turn the grounds into a solid mass of flowers provided you come and live with me. One of my reasons for not letting a landscape gardener near the grounds at Motupipi was that I knew what I wanted— I just didn't know how to go about it. When I looked around your courtyard I had the oddest feeling of coming home, because that was how I wanted the gardens at Motupipi to look.'

'All right.' She kissed him, and smiled to herself as he lifted her high in his arms. When they were married she would talk about the dangers of repressing a vocation. For now, she was content to give him everything she could, make him happier than he had ever been before.

His dark magic had finally ensnared him, too.

ANTONIA sat down with a sigh, pulling off the small-brimmed hat that had shaded her features from the hot spring sun. 'It was a fantastic day,' she said, 'but I'm glad to be home.'

'Are your legs tired?'

She smiled. 'My legs are always tired. I'm turning into a wimp.'

'No, just a pregnant woman.' Philip knelt and pulled her shoes off, then began to knead the tight muscles. She sighed again, voluptuously this time, and wriggled her small feet in his firm, expert hands. 'Stand up,' he murmured.

When she did he stripped off her sheer stockings and extended his ministrations to her calf muscles, his strong fingers easing out the tiredness and the kinks until she groaned with pleasure.

'Too much?' he said, looking up.

Antonia smiled and leaned forward to kiss him. 'No,' she said softly.

One brow rose. His hands slowed, smoothing up behind the sensitive backs of her knees, beneath the soft lemon silk of her skirt, to the warm satin of her thighs. His head was on a level with hers. Antonia felt giddiness threaten as she looked into gold-flecked eyes, saw the lick of flame deep within.

'I thought you were tired.'

'I'm tired,' she said softly, 'not dead.'

He laughed deep in his throat and rose, picking her up effortlessly. 'Then let's take this pretty thing off, and see what you have underneath it,' he said.

Far from dulling her reactions, pregnancy seemed to add new ones, special ones. Perhaps that was why she had decided to have another baby so soon after Nicholas; one of the reasons, anyway, she thought a little smugly as she slid her hand between the buttons of Philip's white shirt and felt that familiar, yet ever fresh, rise of desire.

An hour later she stirred, kissing his shoulder. 'We'd better get up, I suppose.'

'Stay in bed and we'll have dinner together in here.'

She laughed. 'If I'm not too tired to make love, I'm not too tired to get up for dinner. I was so proud of you today, darling.'

His arms tightened around her. 'Were you, my heart? But you're always proud of me.'

'Oh, I'm the perfect wife.'

She expected him to laugh, but his voice was deep and calm and totally unequivocal. 'I don't know whether I tell you often enough, but yes, you are. Perfect for me, all that I have ever wanted, ever needed. I enjoyed today, but the praise and the plaudits meant nothing compared to the smile you gave me. I thought I loved you when we were married, I thought you filled my life, but looking back I can see it was a weak, milk-and-water love that's grown each year until now—well, I suppose I could live without you, but I don't know how.'

Antonia's heart swelled. In the three years of their marriage he had told her every day that he loved her, his face had revealed his love every time he saw her. She should be accustomed to the force and heat and tenderness of his love; but this, on the day when he had been awarded the most prestigious prize for architecture in New Zealand for a house he had designed in Russell, was special.

'It's funny, isn't it?' she said dreamily. 'I feel the same. It seems there are no limits to love. I mean, I love you so much that it seems impossible I could have any to spare, yet when Nicholas was born I fell in love with him, and I suppose I'll do the same in six months' time with this one. No one told me you fell in love with your children.'

She could hear Philip's smile in his voice. 'You're so small to have all this overflowing emotion. I kept looking for you today and all I could see was that ridiculous little hat.'

'It's a very nice hat.' She touched the hard, smooth curve of the muscle in his arm, running her nail through the fine hair. 'I didn't think anyone could ever be this happy,' she confessed. 'Sometimes I wonder whether we're going to have to pay for it.'

His hand came to rest on the spot where their child lay in its protected nest. 'Both of us had fairly rocky childhoods,' he said calmly, 'so I suppose we could say that we've prepaid. But I don't believe that happiness is doled out on a pair of scales. I think we make our own. If you hadn't taken a chance on me, we'd never have reached this place. There are going to be problems, life's full of them, but we'll deal with them together.'

She nodded. Amusement gleamed beneath her lashes. 'I've wondered now and then,' she said with a sly upward glance, 'just what the bequest that your mother made to me was.'

His chest lifted in silent laughter. 'Didn't you guess? It was me.'

Astonishment robbed her of speech for a moment. The tormenting finger that had been roving across his chest stopped. She looked up into his angular face; the dimple flickered in his cheek as he hid his smile. 'Did you tell her?'

'Yes. She was happy because I had found someone to love. That's how it had happened to her, you see. Not so much someone to love her as someone to love. As far as the bequest was concerned——' he shook his head. '—I was still concerned with saving my pride, so I hit on that for an excuse to see you. It wasn't until I got your very snooty letter back that I told pride to go to hell. I realised then that I'd have to bury it and go cap in hand, like a beggar asking for alms.'

'A very arrogant beggar,' she said provocatively, '*demanding* alms. Not that I should have expected anything else; a leopard doesn't change his spots.'

He laughed deep in his throat. 'Does it worry you?'

'No,' she said softly. 'I fell in love with an arrogant, demanding man, but I think I began to love a man with a sneaky dimple that only came to life when he forgot to keep it firmly under control.' She reached up and kissed the place where it hid, still kept under control far too often, although never when he was with her. 'And I learned to love a man who loved his mother, who was loyal and good to his employees, who spent half an hour fixing an old hermit's boat, who'd put his duty to his heritage before his own vocation at heaven knows what psychic cost. A man who could design houses that made my heart sing inside me.'

He moved his head and the kiss fell on to his mouth, hard and searching, yet tender. When it was over he said quietly, 'And I learned to love a woman who was honest enough to stick to her guns in spite of intimidation, but who cared enough about a dying woman to surrender her principles, a woman who set me on fire, yet who was tender and loving, and who told the most awful lies.'

Antonia laughed, and cuddled against him. 'Only one,' she said sleepily. 'And I paid for it, believe me.'

'Go to sleep now, darling.'

His arms tightened. She rested her cheek against his heart, listening to its slow, steady beat with a joy so profound that it brought tears to her eyes. These three years had been the happiest of her life, rich and full and exciting; she could hardly wait for all the other years when she and Philip would be together.

HARLEQUIN®

PRESENTS Plus

Meet Lily Norfolk. Not even her husband's tragic death can convince her to tell his brother, Dane Norfolk, the truth behind their marriage. It's better that he believe she married Daniel for his money and that she had an affair with Daniel's best friend. It's better that Dane keep his distance!

And then there's Elizabeth. She's a respectable young woman, but she also has a secret mission and a secret repressed sensual side. Jake Hawkwood's never liked secrets—he's determined to uncover everything Elizabeth's been hiding....

Lily and Elizabeth are just two of the passionate women you'll discover each month in Harlequin Presents Plus. And if you think they're passionate, wait until you meet Dane and Jake!

Watch for
HOUSE OF GLASS by Michelle Reid
Harlequin Presents Plus #1615
and
THE HAWK AND THE LAMB by Susan Napier
Harlequin Presents Plus #1616

Harlequin Presents Plus
The best has just gotten better!

Available in January wherever Harlequin Books are sold.

WORDFIND #12

```
S  U  C  H  D  A  R  K  M  A  G  I  C  B
A  S  D  F  G  N  R  T  R  U  I  O  P  P
N  Z  X  C  V  T  H  J  A  Y  U  P  L  H
W  E  E  R  T  O  I  L  H  K  G  I  H  I
Q  W  W  E  R  N  J  K  C  L  P  H  E  L
M  N  B  Z  V  I  C  F  G  H  J  S  I  I
I  O  P  U  E  A  T  R  E  W  Q  D  D  P
F  G  H  J  K  A  O  P  T  R  E  N  W  N
A  S  D  F  G  H  L  J  K  L  I  E  O  O
Q  W  E  R  T  Y  U  A  U  I  O  I  P  I
S  T  A  T  I  O  N  S  N  X  C  R  R  S
W  H  J  N  H  F  D  E  R  D  Y  F  O  S
A  Z  X  C  V  B  N  M  K  L  P  I  L  A
R  O  B  Y  N  T  D  O  N  A  L  D  R  P
```

ANTONIA	NEW ZEALAND
CHARM	PASSION
DARK	PHILIP
DONALD	ROBYN
FRIENDSHIP	STATION
MAGIC	SUCH

Join us in January for our trip to Europe—
POSTCARDS FROM EUROPE

WF12

SOLUTIONS TO
WORDFIND #12

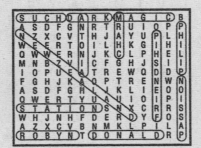

YDU-DA